"Oh!" A small exclamation escaped her parted lips.

The next thing Georgiana knew, she was enveloped in Juan's arms. His lips pried open hers and his tongue played havoc with her senses.

She had been kissed before. But those kisses had consisted of overanxious teenage forays into the new-found realm of petting. Never in the course of her short existence had she experienced anything close to this. Part of her wanted to shove him away in protest. But as his mouth worked on hers, shafts of heat soared and thrust into her pelvis, leaving her limp, weak and moist. Her breasts cleaved to his chest and she felt her nipples harden. Her hands instinctively threaded into his thick black hair and she let out a sigh, giving way to the delicious ardor of her first real kiss.

Fiona Hood-Stewart

AT THE SPANISH DUKE'S COMMAND

Passion™

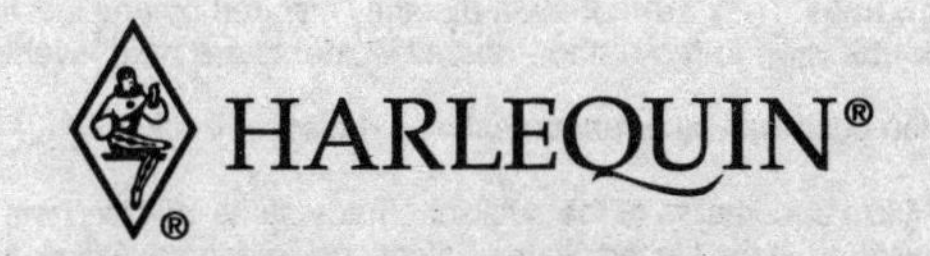

TORONTO • NEW YORK • LONDON
AMSTERDAM • PARIS • SYDNEY • HAMBURG
STOCKHOLM • ATHENS • TOKYO • MILAN • MADRID
PRAGUE • WARSAW • BUDAPEST • AUCKLAND

ISBN 0-373-12448-1

AT THE SPANISH DUKE'S COMMAND

First North American Publication 2005.

This edition published by arrangement with Harlequin Books S.A.

www.eHarlequin.com

Printed in U.S.A.

CHAPTER ONE

AS HIS red Ferrari glided down the wide four-lane Avenida Castellana, Juan Felipe Monsanto, Duque de la Caniza, reflected upon the upcoming autumn and what it held in store. The summer months spent between his yacht and his sumptuous villa in Marbella had gone well. But now it was time to settle a serious matter that could not be delayed any longer: his marriage to Doña Leticia de Sandoval.

As he drew up in front of a grandiose stone building Juan slowed the car and waved amiably to Pepe, the uniformed white-gloved doorman preparing to relieve him of the vehicle.

"*Hola*, Pepe," he said, jumping out of the car and leaving the engine running.

"*Hola, Excellencia*. How was your summer?"

"Great, thank you. Is the Condessa at home?"

"Yes, sir, your aunt is awaiting you."

"Good. I'll call down when I need the car. Have the bags taken up, please."

"Very well, sir." Pepe executed a small bow as Juan entered via the grilled wrought-iron and glass door, crossed the marble lobby and headed for the lift.

It was back to real life now, he reflected. Not that he resented it, or the marriage of convenience that was to take place. This was his destiny. Had been ever since Gregorio, his elder brother, had died in a plane crash five years earlier, leaving Juan heir to the Dukedom. He knew where his duty lay and had no qualms assuming it. Which was why marriage to Leticia de Sandoval was, if not ideal, certainly an acceptable solution. He needed heirs to continue the family bloodline. A wife of suitable lineage was a must. And he respected that.

In fact, he realised, as the lift opened at the top floor and he stepped out onto the lushly carpeted landing and started walking towards his fifteen-room apartment, he considered himself lucky. Leticia de Sandoval was an old family friend, someone who understood the rules of their society as he did. She was an intelligent woman of thirty, and a good lawyer dedicated to many charitable and political causes. She had a life of her own, which suited him just fine.

All in all, he reflected, it was a satisfactory arrangement which would no doubt work out very well. As long as he remained discreet, of course. But that was understood.

Seconds later, as he let himself in through the apartment's front door, Fernando the butler came to welcome him with a smile. "Welcome back, Your Grace. The Condessa is in the small salon waiting for you. May I say, sir, on behalf of the staff and myself, that we are delighted to have you back."

"Thank you, Fernando." Juan handed him his jacket and made his way through to the small salon which the Condessa de Murta favoured. She was the impoverished widow of one of his father's cousins, whom Juan had taken in to keep house. He called her *Tia*—aunt.

"Juan." The elderly woman smiled, silver hair perfectly coiffed, and stretched out a fine white hand. "How lovely to have you back. Have you had a wonderful summer?"

Juan dropped a kiss on her forehead. "Yes, *Tia.* Thank

you. I had a great summer. But now it is time for a reality check. There is much business to attend to. Life returns to normal now that the heat has subsided. Are many people back in town?'' he asked, sitting down opposite her on one of the plump brocade sofas and casually throwing his arm over the back.

''Yes, quite a few,'' the attractive sixty-five-year-old Countess replied, crossing her elegant legs and settling down for a chat with her late husband's young cousin, of whom she couldn't speak well enough. After all, it was he who had offered her a dignified and satisfactory living arrangement when her husband had died leaving her virtually penniless.

''Leticia called. She said to remind you that you have a black tie event tomorrow night at the Zarzuela Palace. Something to do with honouring the benefactors of the orphans of Saint Ignatius. The King and Queen are attending.''

''Which means I must attend,'' Juan said with a rueful smile. ''You realise, of course, that Leticia and I will be getting engaged this autumn, *Tia*?''

''That is excellent news, Juan. I can't tell you how delighted I am. She's such a sensible, intelligent woman, and will make you an excellent wife. She visited yesterday and had tea with me. She brought me some books I'd commented upon. Leticia is always so thoughtful. I did think she looked a little peaky, though. You should tell her not to work so hard.''

''Tell Letti not to work hard?'' Juan laughed, his bronzed features breaking into a wicked smile and his dark eyes flashing. ''That would be impossible. She thrives on work.''

''Nevertheless,'' the Condessa said with a meaningful

look, "she will have to slow down if she intends to have a family."

"Oh, yes, of course. But we won't be married until next spring, so there's time enough to think of all that. Right," he said, ending the discussion and rising, "I'd better go and take a shower and make a few calls. Are you home for dinner?"

"Yes. By the way, Georgiana Cavendish has arrived."

"Georgiana Cavendish?" Juan repeated blankly.

"Really, Juan! Surely you remember? Your late mother's goddaughter, whom we said could stay while she studies Spanish at the university. We discussed it months ago."

"*Dios mio.* Lord and Lady Cavendish's child—of course." He slapped a hand on his brow. "I'd completely forgotten about her."

"Yes. Well, she began her course last Monday. I put her in the Blue Room. I thought it would be appropriate, as it has quite a lot of space and the large desk is satisfactory for her studies."

"That's fine, *Tia*. I'm glad we can help her out."

The Honourable Georgiana Cavendish, only daughter of the late Lord Cavendish and his wife Selina, was thrilled to be in Madrid. At nineteen, with school and a computer course finally behind her, she felt very grown up. Being alone in Madrid was the real thing. The only inconvenience was her mother's insistence that she live at her godmother's son's home rather than in a flat with other students her age, as she would have preferred.

But, considering her mother hadn't wanted her to come to Madrid in the first place, she reckoned she should be thankful for small mercies. Maybe next term she could change her parent's mind. Not that she cared that much.

The Condessa was charming and full of fun, and not having to lift a finger was a plus, she realised, thanking Fernando as he placed her breakfast—a plate of soft scrambled eggs—before her.

Reaching for some toast, Georgiana sighed. It was a week since she'd landed in Madrid, and three days since she'd started her Spanish course at the university—which she was enjoying. But she'd better hurry if she was to catch her bus and be at class on time, she realised, glancing at her watch.

Pouring herself some coffee, Georgiana swept her long golden mane from her face and tucked into a hearty breakfast. But as she raised her fork an interruption made her swivel in her chair. A tall, handsome man in a light grey suit and a yellow silk tie stood eyeing her appraisingly from the doorway.

"Good morning," he said, coming into the room. "I suppose you're Georgiana." He smiled briefly and stretched out his right hand.

"Yes. I am. And I suppose you're the Duke," she answered, matching him look for look. He was much younger than she'd pictured him. Somehow a duke sounded dreadfully stuffy. She'd imagined a pasty-faced middle-aged man. Instead a devastatingly handsome specimen stood before her. When their hands met she experienced an odd tingle. She withdrew hers quickly, struck by the unusual sensation.

"Not 'the Duke'—Juan," he corrected, taking his place at the top of the table. "I hope you are enjoying Madrid," he added politely, signalling Fernando to serve him.

"Very much, thank you." Georgiana's hunger seemed to have disappeared. Why, she could not imagine. He was just her godmother's son, after all, no one special. And her host, she reminded herself, remembering her manners. "It's very kind of you to have me to stay. I hope that next term I won't have to inconvenience you any longer, though. I'll try and find an apartment.''

A slashing dark brow rose haughtily. ''Really? Your mother would approve of such an arrangement?'' Juan asked, taking his first sip of coffee.

''I don't see why not. All my friends share flats in London.''

''Madrid,'' Juan said deliberately, ''is not London.''

''I'm very well aware of that,'' Georgiana responded coldly. Why was he interfering in her affairs? It was none of his damn business if she chose to find a flat.

''In that case you'll do better to reside here during your stay,'' he answered autocratically, accepting a morning paper from the butler.

He skimmed the headlines while Georgiana seethed inwardly. What a high-handed so-and-so! Just because he was a duke, and devastatingly rich and good-looking, it didn't give him the right to interfere in her life. The flashing dark eyes and near-black hair were nothing but a disguise. Underneath he was as stuffy and boring as she'd imagined he would be.

''Ah, I see you've met Juan,'' the Condessa said, entering the breakfast room attired in a pink brocade dressing-gown, her pearls and diamonds already firmly in place.

''Good morning, Condessa. Yes, we've met.'' Georgiana smiled politely at the older woman, then cast Juan a dark look from under her well-shaped brows. ''In fact I was just thanking the Duke for his kind hospitality,'' she said grandly, ''and assuring him that soon I shan't be bothering him any longer.''

He needn't think that just because she was staying here he could run her life. She'd better make that absolutely clear from the word go, she vowed, satisfied, as she finished her eggs, that she'd made her point.

While tacitly avoiding his aunt's comical look of dismay, and pretending to flip through the newspaper, Juan took a good look at his house guest. She was exquisitely beautiful. Long blonde silky hair fell in a straight rush halfway down her back. Her features were classically set, and the little he could see of her figure was superb. She had, he conceded, a beauty that would be hard to match. And that, by his standards, was saying a lot—considering the number of women he'd known over the years.

Despite being shielded by the newspaper, he did not miss the dark look Georgiana cast him from under those superbly etched brows. She also spelled trouble, he reflected with an inner sigh. Any girl as beautiful as this let loose on the streets of Madrid, clad in the clothes she was wearing—low-cut jeans and a T-shirt that barely covered her midriff—would cause traffic jams!

At that moment the phone rang. It was answered by the butler. "For you, Don Juan," Fernando said, handing Juan the mobile phone. "It is Doña Leticia."

"Thank you. Good morning, Letti. How are you? Yes, fine. Just sat down to breakfast. My aunt told me we have that dinner tonight," Juan said, getting up and moving away from the table. "Also we need to have some private time together to settle the details of our engagement."

There was a slight hesitation.

"Letti?"

"Yes, I'm here," she responded. "Perhaps the day after tomorrow? Wait, let me check my diary. No, that won't do, I'm afraid—I have a sit-in at the university to deal with. The law faculty's going through some problems just now, and I promised Pablito Sanchez I'd help him out. Would you mind if we leave it until Sunday?"

"Not at all. That's as good a day as any. In fact, if your parents are around, I might as well pop over to Puerta de Hierro and make an informal *pedido* to your father. I believe it is still customary to ask for a daughter's hand in marriage, even if she is a high-flying professional," he added with a low laugh.

"Yes, I—yes." Leticia answered. "That's fine. We'd better get on with it, I suppose."

"The sooner the better. We've waited long enough as it is. We can discuss when to make the formal engagement announcement with your parents on Sunday."

"Perfect. Be there around twelve for drinks."

"See you then."

Georgiana, whose Spanish was far better than anyone realised, had listened to the call but managed to hide her surprise. Imagine getting engaged to someone in this offhand manner? As though it were a business arrangement. She shuddered inwardly. She had already met Leticia the other day, when she'd visited the Condessa. She'd seemed a nice woman. Not dreadfully exciting or pretty, Georgiana had decided, but charming and very nice.

Oh, well, she figured, folding her napkin and rising from the table, it was Juan's life and none of her business.

"I need to run if I'm going to catch the bus," she exclaimed. "I'm already running late. See you later. Oh, and thanks for the books, Condessa, they're great."

"*De nada*, child. Enjoy your day."

"Thanks." She hesitated a moment as Juan lowered the paper, which he'd resumed reading, and his eyes roamed over her, leaving her blushing.

"If you're late, Jacobo can drive you to the university," he said laconically. Then, before she could protest, he beckoned Fernando. "Please see that the *señorita* is driven to the university every morning, Fernando. It is not suitable for her to be taking public transport.''

''Excuse me?'' Georgiana spluttered, seeing the Condessa's approving smile and remembering the old lady's disparaging comments regarding pubic transport.

''Yes?'' Juan's brow rose once more.

''It's very kind of you to offer me a car, but actually I'd prefer to take the bus. You see—''

''See what?''

''Well, it's more—more fun. I can get more of the flavour of the city, see the way people live and—and all that,'' she ended lamely, hoping she didn't sound ungrateful but determined not to be dominated.

''I'm sure that the past few days have given you an ample perspective of life among the populous, Georgiana. From now on you will go in the car. I have better things to do than worry about your well-being,'' Juan replied peremptorily.

''Worry about my well-being?'' she blurted out. ''Might I point out that I'm nineteen years old, not a child, for goodness' sake. This is ridiculous.'' She turned to the Condessa for support.

''Child, I must say that I have to agree with dear Juan. You never know the dangers that lurk on the streets. Particularly on buses.'' The Condessa shuddered expressively, and raised a linen napkin to her lips.

''But that's absurd!'' Georgiana cried. ''There are no dangers,'' she insisted, feeling the carpet being pulled from under her feet. ''Surely it's not dangerous to take a bus in broad daylight? Everyone else does.''

''You,'' Juan responded firmly, ''are not everyone else. And in those clothes I dread to think what might happen to you.''

"What's wrong with my clothes?" Georgiana demanded, a dangerous glint in her eyes as she drew herself up, a hot, angry flush covering her cheeks.

"They are not proper attire for a young woman attending university."

"Well, of all the—Look—" Georgiana stepped forward, eyes flashing "—everything's been just fine up until now. Why are you determined to interfere?" She faced him head-on.

"I am not interfering," Juan replied calmly. "But while you reside under my roof you will do as I say. We are in Spain, *señorita*, not London. We have certain unwritten rules that we adhere to in our society."

"I've never heard of anything so ridiculous or archaic," Georgiana burst out, despite her efforts to remain polite. "I shall go on the bus if I wish to. Goodbye."

She spun round, picked up the books that were lying on a chair next to the door, and headed towards the hall.

In two quick strides Juan was out of the chair. Before she could take another step into the hall he had manoeuvred so that she was pinned to the wall by his hands on either side of her.

"I would advise you not to do that, *señorita*," he said in a quiet, dangerous voice that left her in no doubt as to his meaning. "I'm a tolerant man, but I don't like spoiled behaviour."

Their eyes met in a duel of wills, hers translucent green, his a dark, piercing chestnut that sent strange shivers coursing through her. His face was only inches away, and for a moment the thought of his lips on hers flashed through her mind. Then reality hit and her chest heaved with righteous anger.

"How dare you?" she muttered, aware that the Condessa and Fernando were interested spectators of the scene.

"How dare you treat me as though I were a child?" Her chin jutted rebelliously.

"If I treated you as a child, my dear, you would already be cooling off in your room," he remarked, eyes gleaming. "I repeat, while you are under my roof you will follow my rules." He moved back and removed his hands, leaving her free to go.

"Oh, how dare you?" Georgiana spluttered, swallowing and trying to compose herself, and not show how shaken she was by his proximity. But his forceful presence, the masterful manner in which he'd ordered her to obey, left her seething.

Without another word she flounced out of the hall and onto the vast landing. Then, not waiting for the lift, she ran down the stairs.

In the main hall she hesitated. She could see a Rolls Royce drawing up, and Pepe preparing to open the door. What should she do? Flout him? Take the bus and risk his anger? Or concede with as much dignity as possible.

For a moment she hesitated, then raising her small determined chin, she plastered on a smile and resolved to make the best of it. She would deal with Juan and his ridiculous autocratic notions when she got home. For now it was better to beat a safe retreat and not make a public spectacle of herself.

Juan watched from the window as she stepped, stiff-backed into the vehicle. A smile hovered about his lips. She was going to be a handful, this one. Oh, well, it was only for a few months, and he probably wouldn't see that much of her. But he'd meant what he said. His rules were his rules. And he would not allow them to be altered.

By her or anyone.

CHAPTER TWO

"So, YOU and Leticia are finally setting a date, are you?" said Don Alvaro de Sandoval, the Marquis de Cabral, his deep, patrician voice laced with satisfaction. A man of medium height and build, he wore a thick curling moustache and sported a head of very white hair.

"Yes, Don Alvaro," Juan replied, accepting a glass of dry sherry from Doña Elvira, Leticia's mother.

"Of course, we don't know exactly when we'll be married," Letti chipped in hastily. "We both have such very busy schedules. It will be hard to find the time to fit in a wedding," she said absently. Tweaking her bobbed brown hair behind her ears, she frowned.

"Why, really, Letti," her mother exclaimed, shocked. "Surely you can both find time for your wedding?"

"Yes, of course, Mother. I didn't mean to sound uninterested." Letti glanced briefly at Juan, who smiled back at her, amused.

Her frankness was one of her best qualities. Neither of them pretended to be in love. It was a practical arrangement that suited them both. He knew that he had a real friend in Letti, and didn't have to pretend to court her. She accepted the arrangement for what it was: a marriage of convenience that suited their time and station in life.

"Don't worry about us, Doña Elvira," he said, placing a reassuring arm on his future mother-in-law's sleeve.

"Letti and I will sort it all out in good time. But I think we can safely say that we are thinking of the spring."

"Exactly. Spring," Letti answered, relieved, straightening the skirt of her chic Chanel tweed suit. "That will give us lots of time to prepare, Mama."

"Well, I hope so," Doña Elvira said doubtfully. "There is always so much to do before a wedding, you know. Remember when Patricia, your sister, got married—all the time it took to decide on the invitations alone? It doesn't bear thinking about."

"I'm sure Juan and I will be able to make up our minds rapidly," she reassured her mother.

"Please don't choose that dreadful recycled paper, will you?" Doña Elvira turned to Juan. "It always looks so grubby. I don't know why people favour it."

"It's ecology, my dear," Don Alvaro assured her. "Good for the environment."

"That's all very well." Doña Elvira sniffed. "But after seeing that dreadful invitation that Teresa Albregon de Lozada sent us the other day I can only shudder. I feel so sorry for her poor mother. It is so ugly I didn't even place it on the mantelpiece in the small drawing room."

"Doña Elvira, I give you my word of honour that no such paper will be used in any shape or form at our wedding." Juan exchanged a quick conspiratorial smile with Leticia while raising Doña Elvira's hand to his lips.

"There. You see, Mama? No need to worry. We'll only settle for something you approve of. In fact, if you like," she said, warming to her theme, "you could choose the invitations yourself. You wouldn't mind that, would you, Juan? It would save a lot of trouble," she added in an under-voice.

"Really, Letti!" her mother exclaimed, brows raised.

"I'm ashamed of you. Not choose your own wedding invitations, indeed! I never heard of anything so preposterous."

"Very well, Mama." Leticia sighed, rolled her eyes and smiled at Juan once more. "You pick out those you like the best, Mama, and we'll select one of them."

Hoping she'd appeased her parent, at least for the moment, Leticia went with Juan out onto the terrace, where they sat for a while in wide wicker chairs, enjoying the early autumn day while they sipped their drinks. The house, in the distinguished Madrid suburb of Puerta de Hierro, had a huge private garden and a lovely lawn. Two peacocks preened themselves by the lily pond, their splayed feathers caught in the fleeting sunlight.

"So, how are things going now that you're back?" Letti asked, leaning back and watching Juan.

"Fine. Business as usual. By the way, I meant to tell you—the Mondragales send you their best. I had drinks with them before leaving Marbella. They hope to be here later in the season."

"Good. They're very nice. And, of course, a *very* interesting contact for that paper business of yours," she pointed out with a significant look.

"Great minds think alike. I can already tell what an excellent wife you'll be, Letti." He laughed, appreciating how quick on the uptake she was. "And you're absolutely right. Alberto Mondragal is the ideal chap to take on board. I think he's definitely very interested..."

"Then remind me to organise a small dinner party when they're in town," Letti said, in her practical down-to-earth way. "How's your house guest getting on, by the way? I met her the other day, when I was visiting your aunt. She seemed a delightful girl."

"Georgiana? Delightful?" Juan's brows came together

in a thick line above the ridge of his patrician nose. "She's a perfect little pest. Why the Condessa ever consented to having her come and stay is beyond me."

"Well, she asked you and you agreed. I remember. I was there. It was your mother's wish," Leticia added softly, hoping that the reminder of the parent he'd lost last year was not too painful.

"I know. And that is the only reason I haven't sent her packing back to England already. I can't imagine how Lady Cavendish could be so lax with her daughter."

"What do you mean?"

"It appears the girl is allowed a ridiculous amount of freedom. She comes and goes pretty much as she pleases."

"Well," Letti responded reasonably, "she's over eighteen, you know. Not an infant."

"That still doesn't make it appropriate for her to be gallivanting around the city in jeans that barely cover her bottom and— Well, I won't get into it."

"But they all dress like that nowadays, Juan. It's not like it was back in our day. You should see some of Pablito Sanchez's students at the law school. I'm sure Georgiana is positively prim next to them." She laughed.

"You may be right," he conceded, smiling, "but it still doesn't meet with my approval. I suppose I have very old-fashioned notions."

"Completely outdated, *querido*," she responded complacently. "Let's hope that by the time your own children grow up you'll have got used to the inevitable changes ahead," she said, her rich, soft laugh filling the air.

"Who knows what they'll be wearing by then?" he agreed. The sudden vision of children of his own was somewhat daunting. "Oh, I think your mother's beckoning us for lunch," he continued, rising, glad to change the subject. "By the way, I thought it all went off quite well with your parents, didn't you, *querida*?'' He linked his arm with hers in a friendly manner.

''Oh, very well,'' she agreed. ''Mama will be quite satisfied to have the run of the wedding in the end. Thank goodness,'' she murmured, laughing. ''I really can't spare the time.''

''No. Of course not,'' Juan answered.

But as they entered the dining room he couldn't quell a slight feeling of disappointment. He was no romantic, but wasn't a woman supposed to be a tiny bit excited about her forthcoming nuptials?

Telling himself not to be ridiculous, that he was very lucky to be marrying such a sensible, altogether suitable young woman, Juan sat down on his hostess's right and set about charming her through lunch.

''He's insufferable,'' Georgiana exclaimed to the Condessa as they sat sipping *orchata* in the living room. ''I don't know why you let him get away with it.''

''But what is wrong with a man seeing to one's every comfort?'' the Condessa enquired uncomprehendingly. ''I am only too grateful to Juan for all his attentions. You know, it's thanks to him that I'm able to live in this gracious manner. Such a dear boy,'' she murmured, a fond sigh escaping her.

Georgiana was about to make a pithy response when she realised it would be rude and undignified to criticise her host further. She'd already had a row about it with her mother on the phone. Lady Cavendish had flatly refused to allow Georgiana to move into a flat with two American girls from San Francisco. If she wished to remain in Spain then she would do so at the Duque de la Caniza's residence or not at all. Georgiana was still fuming from the conversation, which she'd just relayed in injured tones to the

Condessa. But, although she'd listened sympathetically to Georgiana's complaints, the Condessa had offered no solutions.

It really was becoming unbearable.

Well, never mind, Georgiana reflected, cheering up. Tonight she was going out on a date with a chap she'd met in the university cafeteria, who was studying art and had a Porsche. He seemed fun, and hung out with a cool group of kids. The fact that he had a pierced tongue didn't deter her in the least.

Juan was due back later tonight, the Condessa told her, from a trip to Seville where he'd been for a couple of days. So much the better. At least she could breathe freely when he wasn't around. For some reason she could not explain she seemed uptight whenever he came near. Which just went to prove how domineering and insufferable he was. Otherwise why would he provoke such a reaction in her?

At eight o' clock the downstairs bell rang and Fernando answered. "It's for you, *señorita.* Someone is waiting for you downstairs."

"Thanks, Fernando. Don't wait up. I have my key."

"But, *señorita*, you won't be too late?"

"Of course not," she replied blithely. "But in case I am, don't worry."

"Very well, *señorita.*" The manservant opened the front door for her and Georgiana, dressed in low-slung black Gucci pants and a short, clinging, and very fashionable white top, got into the lift. When it arrived at the lobby she stopped, horrified, when the doors opened and Juan stood before her.

"Hello," she said, doing a double take and swallowing nonchalantly. He looked dark, handsome and forbidding, standing there at the entrance of the lift.

"Good evening, Georgiana. Do I gather you are going out?"

"That's right. Some friends from college." Why she felt nervous when she had every right to go out was beyond her.

"And what time do you plan to be back?"

"Oh, I don't know." She waved an airy hand. "Whenever."

"I see. Well, have a good evening."

With a slight bow and without a smile he stood aside for her to pass. Why, she wondered, annoyed, did she feel as if he'd stripped her naked? For an instant she almost wished she could cover herself. Then, straightening her shoulders, she forced herself to walk in a self-assured sexy manner through the lobby, down the steps and into the waiting Porsche.

Juan watched as the car roared into the evening traffic. Then he unclenched his fist, wondering why it should irritate him so profoundly to see Georgiana take off with that uncouth-looking creature with a pierced tongue. Heaven help his kids if this was what lay in store for them.

Pressing the button in the lift, he thought about Georgiana, annoyed at his sudden physical reaction. "Damn the girl," he muttered under his breath, consigning the sudden slash of heat coursing straight to his groin to the devil. He had no right to have any thoughts about her at all—except, perhaps, the proper concern due to a young woman at present under his protection. So why had he felt an irresistible desire to push her against the elevator wall and kiss her very thoroughly, rather than watch her walk out through the front door?

Closing his eyes a moment, Juan took a deep breath and reminded himself that not only was he engaged to be married, but that any extramarital affairs must be conducted with older women who knew the name of the game. Preferably married ones who were utterly discreet. Not vulnerable sexy teenagers.

By the time he reached the apartment, and Fernando had ushered him in, Juan was back in control. The ridiculous moment of sexual weakness—something any man might experience when placed before a beautiful, seductive young woman—had passed. But in the future he vowed there would be no more such moments.

Not if he could help it.

CHAPTER THREE

JUAN woke at the second ring of the phone next to his bed. Groggily he switched on the bedside lamp. Then he glanced at the clock. *Dios mio*, it was four a.m. Who on earth could be calling him at this hour?

"Dígame?" he said, brows meeting in surprise over the ridge of his nose as he sat up abruptly. Calls in the middle of the night never spelled anything good.

"Am I speaking to His Grace the Duke of Caniza?" a deep voice asked.

"You are," Juan replied warily, his attention fully focused now.

"This is the police."

"The police?" He was fully alert.

"Yes. We have a young English lady here by the name of Georgiana Cavendish." The officer pronounced the name with difficulty. "She claims to be staying at your address."

"That is correct," Juan replied stiffly. "What is she doing in your station?"

"There has been a traffic incident," the officer answered lugubriously. "The young man she was with was speeding on the Avenida Generalissimo. He was stopped and breathalysed."

"But no one was hurt?" He felt a familiar rush of anxiety.

"No, Your Grace. Both are fine."

"I see. Then why is Miss Cavendish being held?"

"She's not. But as I understand the girl is under your protection, *Excellencia*, I didn't think it would be appropriate—"

"She's not a minor. She's nineteen years old," he snapped.

"I know, *Excellencia*, but a young girl like that shouldn't be out on her own with wild young men who are driving under the influence," the officer said repressively. "I am a father myself, of two daughters. I felt it was my duty to inform whoever is in charge of her."

"Quite right, Officer. Thank you," Juan replied dryly. "I suppose you wish me to come and pick her up?"

"Well, sir, I think that under the circumstances that would be best."

"Very well. Please inform Miss Cavendish that I shall be there in under half an hour."

Juan hung up the phone and, swearing under his breath, went to the bathroom, where he splashed cold water over his face. Damn it, he should have known this would end in trouble. Dragging on a pair of jeans, a shirt and some loafers, he grabbed his tan suede jacket and his car keys and headed down to the basement garage.

His anger towards Georgiana smouldered as the lift descended. She was a pest, a thorough nuisance, and the sooner she packed her bags and left Madrid the happier he would be.

Minutes later the Ferrari roared down the half-empty Paseo de la Castellana towards the address of the police station the officer had given him.

By the time he walked into the unprepossessing building his temper had risen another few notches. The sight of Georgiana sitting sulkily on a wooden bench did nothing to abate it.

Ignoring her, Juan spoke directly with the officer in charge.

"I'm very sorry that you have been caused so much trouble, Officer," he said, flashing his most charming smile.

"Oh, it's not too serious, *Excellencia.* Not for her, anyway. The young man is a different matter. These young people with fast sports cars are all the same." The older man shook his head. "Irresponsible, I'm afraid. I blame the parents," he continued with a sigh. "And if I may be permitted to say so, *Excellencia,*" he added, lowering his voice, "you'd be wise to keep an eye on her in future. A pretty girl like that let loose on the town can only cause trouble," he murmured in a man-to-man tone.

"My sentiments exactly," Juan answered. "Now, if you'll allow me, Officer, I shall relieve you of this bothersome charge."

Georgiana, who'd been listening to the interchange, underwent an immediate change of attitude. She'd felt ashamed, then embarrassed, then grateful to Juan for rescuing her. Now, as he turned and looked her over with that arrogant, possessive stare, she wished she'd never mentioned his wretched name. She sent him a hostile glare. It would have been far preferable to spend a night in jail than be subjected to his insufferable manners.

"Come on," he said, without so much as a smile. "You've caused enough bother around here for one evening."

Then he turned to the officer and took his leave, making Georgiana feel like a recalcitrant schoolgirl being shepherded out of the headmistress's office by an angry parent. But since there was no alternative she obeyed reluctantly, walking before him to the Ferrari parked on the kerb, her head held high. Serve him right if he got a ticket, she reflected sourly, slamming the door as she got in, her previous gratitude to him fading completely as Juan's forbidding figure entered the vehicle.

Georgiana sat staring straight ahead.

Juan didn't say a word, merely gunned the engine and drove off at a sedate pace down the wide avenue. If only he'd explode, at least then she could rave back at him, Georgiana reflected grudgingly. Nothing could be worse than this dreadful silence.

Out of the corner of her eye she took a peek at him. He looked stern and she swallowed.

Then all at once the vehicle came to a stop in front of a café that appeared open despite the early hour.

''Get out,'' Juan commanded once he'd parked the vehicle.

''I don't want to get out,'' Georgiana demurred, stubbornly crossing her arms. ''I'm tired. I want to go home.''

''I don't wish to repeat myself, Georgiana,'' Juan murmured dangerously.

''I—''

''Haven't I made myself clear?'' he enquired, in a low, menacing tone that left her in no doubt that should she not obey he would find a way of making her.

It went against the grain, but slowly she exited the car, and with as much dignity as she could muster entered the café.

Soon they were seated at a table. Juan ordered in quick Spanish. And, despite her wish to stay cool and indifferent, Georgiana realised that she was more shocked by the incident that had occurred than she cared to show. All at once she realised just how cold and hungry she was. The order of *chocolate con churros*—delicious hot chocolate and the deep-fried fritters dipped in sugar that she'd learned to love in the past few weeks—would be very welcome and comforting. A sudden rush of tears burned her eyes as weariness and fright hit her unexpectedly. She swallowed and turned quickly away, determined not to show weakness.

Juan was about to give Georgiana a harsh talking-to when he noted her hands, clenched and white, trembling in her lap. He glanced at her face, partially hidden by the long silky mane. The sight of a single tear rolling down her cheek made him sigh.

And just as his anger had flared so it abated.

She was, after all, a very young girl with little experience of life. What had happened to her was no different from what happened to many other young people, and it would merely serve as a lesson. A smile hovered about his lips and tenderness surged. He slipped a hand over her trembling fingers.

"Now, now, *querida*, don't be upset. What happened was stupid and unnecessary, but it's over," he said softly.

Georgiana sniffed and Juan removed a large white pocket handkerchief from his jacket. Slipping his hand under her chin, he turned her face towards him. God, she was lovely, he realised with a jerk. Beautifully, deliciously lovely. Those huge green eyes were tearful and misty, her breasts heaving as she tried to control her distress.

Juan got up and went around the table to sit next to her. "There, there," he said, wiping the tears with his hanky, "*No llores, cariña.* Please don't cry. It's all right." He slipped a reassuring arm around her shoulders and drew her head onto his shoulder. "Let it out and stop worrying. You're safe now."

Georgiana could hardly believe his words, or the extraordinary sensation of relief she experienced when Juan's arm came about her and her cheek rested on his taut muscled shoulder. It only made her want to cry harder. She gulped, took the hanky from him and blew her nose, unable to believe this was the same man who half an hour ago had picked her up at the police station.

''I'm really t-terribly s-sorry to have caused you so much trouble,'' she gulped. ''I woke you up in the middle of the night,'' she added in a muffled whisper into his shirt-front.

''Shush. Look, here are the *churros* and the chocolate. Now, sit up and have some. You'll feel better.'' Gently he drew her up. ''Eat this,'' he said, dipping a sugar-coated *churro* into the piping hot, thick dark chocolate, then holding it close for her to eat.

''Thank you.'' Georgiana swallowed, heaved a shaky sigh, and nibbled. It was warm and comforting, and all at once she began to feel better. ''I really am sorry,'' she said between bites, determined to expiate her sin.

''I know,'' he murmured, a smile hovering. ''You've told me several times. Now, drink your chocolate and stop worrying. It's over. Just make sure it doesn't happen again,'' he said with mock severity, the twinkle in his eyes belying his tone.

Georgiana smiled at last. ''You've been so decent about all this.'' She hesitated, then looked deep into his eyes. ''You—you won't tell the Condessa—or my mother?'' she begged in a tentative tone.

''That depends on how you plan to behave in the future,'' he answered, a speculative grin forming on his handsome face.

''But that's blackmail!'' Georgiana exclaimed, nearly dropping the *churro*, his comment jolting her back to her old self as he'd intended. ''That's outrageous. You're going to hold this over me like a—a—''

''Sword of Damocles?'' he enquired helpfully.

''Exactly. You can't do that,'' she muttered hotly.

''Can't I?'' The speculative smile deepened.

''Absolutely not. It's outrageous.''

Did she have any idea how perfectly lovely she was? Those bright green eyes were filled with the remains of tears and righteous anger, her breasts, outlined by the tight T-shirt, thrust out unwittingly as she flounced at him. All at once, unable to resist, Juan snaked his hand behind her neck and drew her to him.

''Oh!'' A small exclamation escaped her parted lips. The next thing she knew she was enveloped in Juan's well-worked-out arms. His lips prised open hers, and his tongue played havoc with her senses.

Georgiana had been kissed before. But those kisses had consisted of over-anxious teenage forays into the new-found realm of petting. Never, in the course of her short existence, had she experienced anything close to this. Part of her wanted to shove him away, protest. But as his mouth worked on hers shafts of heat soared and thrust into her pelvis, leaving her limp, weak and moist. Her breasts cleaved to his chest and she felt her nipples harden. Her hands instinctively threaded into his thick black hair and she let out a sigh, giving way to the delicious ardour of her first real kiss.

Then, just as he had taken her, he pulled away.

''Dios mio!'' he exclaimed, dragging his fingers through his hair and signalling the waiter for the bill.

Still recovering from the whirlwind sensations, Georgiana watched silently as he paid. Then, before she had time to regroup, he grabbed her arm and marched her firmly out of the café.

''Juan—I—what happened?''

''Something that never should have.'' He stopped abruptly, placed his hands on her shoulders and stood her away from him. ''Stay out of my way, Georgiana. For your own good.''

"But, what—?"

"Don't. It was my fault. I should never have done that. I'm sorry." Then without another word he walked to the car, opened the door for her punctiliously, then, once she was inside, closed it.

They drove home in heavy silence.

Juan seethed inwardly, furious at himself for giving way to temptation. He had no business kissing this girl. He was about to become engaged to Leticia. This girl was staying in his house—under his protection. It was unthinkable.

When they finally reached the building, and parked in the garage, Georgiana stepped shakily out of the car. Then they boarded the elevator and rode it in complete silence. On the top-floor landing Juan unlocked the apartment door carefully. No one was about.

"Go to your room quickly," he whispered.

"Juan, can't we talk about what happened?" Georgiana whispered back.

"There is nothing to talk about. I made a mistake. I'm sorry. Forget it. Now, go to bed and get some sleep," he commanded.

Reluctantly Georgiana slipped down the wide corridor and carefully opened the door to her room. Inside, she flopped on the bed and sighed, still trying to assimilate all that occurred during the course of the evening. But all that stuck was the lasting sensation of Juan's lips on hers.

Finally closing her eyes and pulling the covers over her, Georgiana crawled into bed and allowed sleep to overtake her. But even as she dreamed a new awareness took hold. Something deep within her had changed.

And she liked it.

Juan entered the study and poured himself a stiff whisky. *Por Dios,* where was his head at? How could he have been so irresponsible? He'd actually kissed Georgiana. At the thought of the kiss he dropped into the worn leather armchair that had belonged to his late father and let out a groan. He leaned back, closed his eyes and sighed. It was years since he'd felt anything like it—years since he'd experienced that unique coiling sensation of delight as his lips touched a woman's.

And there had been many women.

But until tonight there had been none to replace Leonora, the lovely young girl he'd once loved and who'd been wrenched from him so suddenly in a terrible boat crash one summer, when she was holidaying with her family in Ibiza. Taking a gulp of whisky, he drummed his fingers on the arm of the chair. Just thinking of Leonora still had the power to hurt him, even though the accident had occurred twelve years ago. And tonight Georgiana's soft, compliant lips, resistant at first, then melting so deliciously, and the tender, spontaneous gesture of her fingers threading his hair had left him undone.

Sitting up, Juan pulled himself together.

It was absurd. Ridiculous.

He was reacting like a teenager, not a man of thirty. Perhaps he should call Leticia tomorrow and suggest they bring forward the wedding. The sooner he got married and settled the better. He shook his head and let out a harsh, disparaging laugh at himself. How could he—a veteran, a man who'd had his share of experience, who knew women like the back of his hand—be caught unawares by a simple kiss?

Closing his eyes once more, Juan groaned as the memory of Georgiana's nipples hardening against his chest caused another flame of heat to flash straight to his groin. *Dios*, this was unbearable.

Then abruptly he rose and, turning out the lights, headed

to his room. Tomorrow he would take measures to curtail this absurd business. But all that would help his present state, he reflected wryly, was a very cold shower.

The next day being Saturday, it was close to noon by the time Georgiana finally woke up. As she stretched and opened her eyes the previous night's adventures surfaced.

"Oh, dear," she muttered, feeling the button of her pants squeezing her tummy. She hadn't even undressed.

Climbing stiffly out of bed, she headed to the bathroom and stared at her face. Smeared mascara and rumpled hair was not a pretty sight. She grimaced at herself and, throwing off her clothes, walked into the huge marble shower, letting the hard water jets wake her sleepy body. As she did so the previous evening rolled out in slow motion, including the unexpected finish.

How, she wondered, lathering the soap, had she ended up in Juan's arms? And how could it have felt so very wonderful to be there? It was crazy. Juan. The man she'd come to loathe, who was so much older than her—a man who never would have crossed her mind as anything but an odious figure of authority. Yet now, as the water trickled down her back, her nipples hardened and a delicious hitherto unknown sensation pulsated between her thighs at the thought of him.

Turning off the water abruptly, Georgiana stepped out of the shower and wrapped herself in one of the soft white terry cloth monogrammed towels. As she did so she thought of Leticia.

Oh, no. How awful. Poor Leticia, who had been so welcoming and nice to her. How could she have allowed such a thing to happen?

Feeling like a Jezebel, Georgiana perched on the edge of the vast bathtub and wallowed in an attack of guilt. She must get away from here. She couldn't possibly stay under the same roof as Juan after what had occurred. She simply must find a way of persuading her mother to allow her to go into a flat.

On this determined note Georgiana rose and returned to the bedroom to get dressed. She would slip out of the house and spend the day somewhere—anywhere but here.

CHAPTER FOUR

"THAT was not too bad, all things considered," Leticia said once she and Juan were ensconced in the back of the Rolls Royce and being driven by Juan's chauffeur, Jacobo.

"No. For an evening of speeches and mediocre food, I suppose it wasn't," Juan agreed, laughing, loosening his satin bow-tie, which he left hanging around his neck, and reaching for Leticia's hand. "You'll be a great duchess, Letti. A credit to the family, mark my words. You're wonderful at looking interested when people are boring you stiff."

"Rubbish!" she exclaimed, giving his hand a friendly squeeze. "I'm used to listening to people. It's part of a lawyer's job."

"Certainly a dedicated, socially conscious lawyer like you," he replied in a more serious tone. "When are you going to the conference on abused women's rights?"

"Next week. Tuesday night. At the university. Will you come?"

"Of course. I'll be interested to hear your views."

"You may not entirely approve of them," she murmured ruefully as the car drew up in front of the sleek apartment block on Velazquez where she lived.

"I may surprise you yet. I have great respect for women, and detest the idea of any woman being mistreated."

"I know you do," she replied affectionately. Then, as

the car slowed, she dropped a kiss on his cheek. "I won't ask you in for a nightcap as I have to be in court at eight o'clock." She grimaced.

Juan hesitated, then, leaning over, drew her into his arms. "Surely we could do a good deal better than this, Letti? After all, in a few months we'll be married." He looked down into her eyes, and frowned when he saw a wary restraint enter them. He had no desire to frighten her, but she was a thirty-year-old woman after all. He'd naturally presumed that over the years she must have acquired some kind of sexual experience. Yet the way she went stiff in his arms was anything but encouraging. "Sorry," he said, drawing back, his tone stiff. "I didn't mean to offend you in any manner."

"You don't bother me in the least, Juan," Leticia said, embarrassed. "It's just that I have to get up early, and it's late, and I—"

"Of course." He cut her short, smiled perfunctorily and got out of the car to see her to the door. "I'll give you a ring tomorrow. Perhaps we can get together at the weekend?"

"Yes," she said, sounding relieved. "That would be lovely. We could take in a round of golf and have dinner at the Club."

"Perfect." He dropped a chaste kiss on her forehead and watched as she entered the marble-halled building with a wave.

But as he was driven the rest of the way home Juan frowned again. What was it about Letti that wasn't right? She was always obliging and friendly. They were at ease in each other's company. So what had made her draw back when he tried to kiss her? A sudden flash of Georgiana, whom he hadn't seen since the fateful incident the week before, made him swallow. He let out a muffled oath and told the chauffeur to drop him a couple of blocks from his home. He needed to walk.

As he arrived at the front door of the building the night porter opened up.

"*Buenas noches*, Don Juan."

"*Buenas noches*, Julio." Juan smiled at the man, then made his way to the lift. On reaching the apartment he entered quietly and headed straight down the wide carpeted corridor, lit by small bronze picture lights which illuminated the art gracing the walls. When he reached Georgiana's room he stopped. He saw a sliver of light seeping from below the door and hesitated. Just as he was about to move on the door opened.

"Oh!" Georgiana jumped.

"I'm sorry." Juan stepped back immediately.

"I—I was going to the kitchen to get a glass of water," she stammered, blushing. This was their first encounter since the night he'd kissed her. Georgiana swallowed, enveloped by a sudden rush of heat.

"I was just passing on the way to my room," he said stiffly.

"Ah, yes, of course." Georgiana smiled weakly. He looked so handsome, with his hair slightly dishevelled, his bow-tie lying negligently on the white shirt-front, the jacket of his tux casually opened.

Then all at once, as though sensing her discomfort, he smiled. "Come," he said winningly. "A glass of water is a good idea. I'll join you. Though I fear my nightcap will be a brandy."

She smiled back tentatively, then together they walked back down the corridor, across the hall and into the kitchen. Georgiana headed for the cupboard. She removed a glass, and Juan was ready with a bottle of chilled mineral water he'd taken from the fridge. He filled the glass carefully.

"There. Now we can make ourselves comfortable in the study."

He held the door for her and she passed through, willing the churning sensations she was experiencing to quieten down. She tugged her nightgown, wishing rather wistfully that she was wearing flowing silk rather than graceless flannel stamped with images of Winnie the Pooh. Though of course she shouldn't care what she looked like, she admonished herself severely as they entered the study and Juan poured himself a brandy from the decanter. After all, the man was engaged to be married to another woman.

Sitting on the deep couch near the fireplace, Georgiana curled her toes beneath her among the cushions.

"*Salud.*" Juan raised the brandy snifter and sat in the armchair opposite, at a suitable distance.

"*Cheers,*" she said, a smile curving her lips as she raised her glass of water.

"I think we need a fire," Juan said, getting up and lighting the logs already set in the hearth. Soon the pleasant crackle of flames filled the air.

Georgiana let out a tiny sigh and relaxed, feeling at ease with him again, as though the kissing incident hadn't taken place. Though of course it had, she reminded herself, trying to convince herself she wouldn't want it to happen again.

"So. Tell me about your classes," Juan said, leaning back in the soft leather chair and taking a long swig of brandy. Georgiana, he realised with a touch of dry humour, had not the faintest idea how deliciously sexy she looked in her long flannel nightgown, her hair falling about her shoulders, the tiny moist film over her top lip as she sipped the water just asking to be removed. The sudden desire to kiss it away made him sit up straighter and take another quick sip of brandy.

"It's fine," she was saying. "We're beginning to study some literature. *Romancero Gitano*."

"Ah. Federico García Lorca. One of our great poets, executed by the Fascists during the civil war."

"Yes. It's beautiful verse."

Juan smiled and recited part of a poem.

"You know Lorca by heart?" she exclaimed, surprised.

"I'm fond of poetry."

"So am I," she said, and their eyes met in a shared moment of complicity. Then Georgiana looked quickly away and finished her water. "I suppose I'd better go back to bed. It's getting late."

"Already? Shall I get you some more water?" Juan rose, moving lithely to where she stood, hovering and unsure whether to leave or stay.

"I don't think—"

He removed the glass from her hand.

He shouldn't—mustn't. But the need was too strong.

Lightly he touched her cheek. "You are too lovely for your own good," he murmured hoarsely, enchanted not just by her sensuous beauty but by the sensitive creature he intuitively perceived her to be just below the surface. Then, unable to resist, he drew her into his arms.

This time, regardless of all her noble resolutions, Georgiana did not resist. Like a magnet, a mesmerising force was drawing her in, and despite every good intention not to, she succumbed. Slowly Juan's lips came purposefully down on hers, prying them open. As his arms enveloped her, his hands stroked up and down her back, pulling her to him until she felt the hardness of his desire. Another torrent of emotion splintered through her body. Heat rushed to her cheeks, her breast, her abdomen, and she melted between her thighs. As the kiss deepened, and his body cleaved to hers, she let out a little moan.

"*Linda,*" he whispered, taking her down with him onto the sofa and laying her back amongst the cushions, "*Mi Linda.*"

Georgiana could no more walk away than she could resist. Her entire being felt deliciously on fire, her nipples two sensitive peaks, her core a throbbing, anticipating chalice of pent-up desire. When Juan's tantalising fingers finally reached her aching nipples, gently grazing them through the soft flannel nightdress, she threw her head back and let out a low gasp of delight, arching towards him as he taunted her further, guiding her expertly towards the brink.

Now, as Juan gazed down at her, arching in his arms, he knew instinctively that it was the first time Georgiana had experienced anything like this. It was too late to go back, too late to stop, he realised, knowing he couldn't even if he'd wanted to. Gently he lifted her nightdress and drew it over her head, revelling in her creamy-skinned body lying naked before him, etched in the soft glow of the flames.

"You are beautiful," he whispered, lowering his head to her breast while his fingers caressed her legs, travelling upwards until he reached her inner thigh.

For an instant he hesitated, knowing that what he was doing was wrong, that he should not be here with this girl. But it was too late. As his fingers discovered the soft, moist honey between her thighs he groaned and gave way to the delicious intense sensation of bringing her to orgasm. Slowly he reconnoitered, let his thumb graze the tiny nub of flesh until she arched and cried for fulfilment. Now he laved and teased her nipples further as she arched again, begging for release. But still he carried on, driving her to a peak, until in one thrusting movement she let out a cry of joy. He muffled it with his lips and she fell back, trembling.

When he felt her go limp in his arms, Juan drew her carefully to him, held her close. And together they shared a long intimate moment of joy where nothing was present but their shared pleasure.

Little by little Georgiana came slowly back to earth. Never had she experienced anything remotely similar. Now, as she lay quietly naked in Juan's arms, her head resting against the breast pocket of his dinner jacket, breathing the scent of his aftershave, she felt as though a window had opened and a new part of her life had begun. Instinctively she reached her hand up and touched his cheek.

The tenderness of the gesture shocked him back to life. Made him realise how entirely irresponsible and wrong he'd been to permit things to go this far. He had no right to let this young woman fall in love with him—as he sensed from her tender gesture she would—had no right to take her innocence and betray his future wife inside the portals of his home where, within a few months, Leticia would be residing.

Placing Georgiana's hand gently back in her lap, he picked up the flannel nightgown and slipped it over her head. Georgiana struggled to get her arms in and he smiled. She was part-child, part-woman—the most lovely, desirable creature he'd ever met. Yet she was out of bounds and he must not forget it.

She sighed and smiled up into his face. Juan felt a rush of guilt.

"Georgiana, what happened here tonight shouldn't have," he said bluntly.

She nodded, swallowed. "I know. What are we going to do?" she asked in a small voice, looking to him for guidance.

''There is nothing to be done, I'm afraid,'' he replied harshly, getting up and pacing the room. ''You must forgive me for having taken advantage of your innocence and forget I exist. I had no business seducing you. As you well know, I'm engaged to be married. This was out of line.''

''But it happened all the same,'' Georgiana protested, hurt pride coming to her rescue. ''We both knew the circumstances before. I'm not a child, you know. I can take responsibility. If this—if this has happened,'' she said, a delicious flush covering her cheeks, ''it's because we both wanted it to. Doesn't that count for something?''

He stopped pacing and looked down at her, hearing the truth of her words. In a gentler voice he replied. ''It should, *cariña*. But unfortunately it is not to be. We must resist this temptation. As for blame, the only guilty party here is me. You are not to feel at fault. I am eleven years your senior—a man of the world. I should have known better than to take advantage of you. Particularly when you are residing under my roof,'' he added, disgusted.

''Oh, no, we're not back at that again, are we?'' Georgiana said, his words causing a surge of anger. ''We both knew we shouldn't do it, but we did. Well, it may have been wrong. But is it wrong for two people to feel so intensely drawn to each other?'' she questioned, her small chin jutting out, her huge eyes seeking the truth in his.

Juan dragged his fingers through his rumpled hair. ''Yes. No. It is not wrong to feel what we felt. It is the circumstances that are wrong.''

''I agree,'' Georgiana said, making a dignified retreat. All she'd needed to know was that he'd felt the same way she had. ''I will make arrangements to leave the house as soon as possible.''

''Absolutely not,'' he said harshly. ''You will stay here. It is I who will leave. I have to go on several business trips anyway. Plus I have another place here in town—a bachelor pad I can stay at. I will tell the Condessa that I'm very busy. She'll understand,'' he added ironically.

''How about Letti?'' she challenged. ''Will she understand?''

''Yes. Oh, she will never suspect that anything went on between us,'' he said, an ironic twist to his lips. ''She'll just think I'm having an affair with an actress or some new model and turn her eyes the other way.''

''And is that really what you want out of marriage?'' Georgiana asked, her brows meeting in a frown. ''How can you think of marrying a woman you don't love and who doesn't love you? For if she loved you,'' Georgiana threw hotly, ''she would never tolerate that kind of behaviour.''

Juan looked at her, eyes arrested. ''You mean *you* wouldn't tolerate it?'' he asked, suddenly curious.

''No. Of course I damn well wouldn't. I think it's appalling.''

''What does a child like you know of marriage?'' he said with a bitter laugh. ''It is not a passion we're talking about, but a contract.''

''Is that how you think of marriage? As a contract?''

''Yes. That is how it should be, and how it will be with Leticia and myself. That is what our place in society demands.''

''Then you're welcome to it,'' Georgiana threw back. ''I think you're the biggest hypocrite on earth, Juan Monsanto. May you enjoy your loveless marriage and long may it last.''

With that she spun on her heel and, head high, closed the door behind her with a bang, leaving Juan swearing aimlessly before the fire, unable to do more than wish his life was not such a damn mess.

CHAPTER FIVE

"JUAN, you're not concentrating on your game," Leticia rebuked affectionately as Juan's golfball disappeared into a neighbouring bunker. "I've never seen you play so badly. Where's that one-digit handicap disappeared to?" Her forehead creased as she looked at him enquiringly. "Is something the matter?" she asked solicitously, brushing back her chestnut hair and observing him closely. He'd looked strangely drawn these past few days. She wondered if he had a business problem.

"Damn," Juan muttered, following the ball's unfortunate trajectory.

"If you like we can call it a day," Leticia offered reasonably. "After all, we've played nine holes and we should be getting back for lunch. I have a memo to prepare this afternoon."

"What, on a Sunday?" Juan asked, distracted.

"Yes. I'm afraid I have so much on my plate at the moment. Pablito Sanchez is up to his eyeballs at the university, and I promised I'd help out. It's the conference on abused women. You know—the one I told you about?"

"Yes. But surely you can take one whole day off a week?"

"I would if I could," Leticia said regretfully. "But seeing as I have to squeeze in the engagement party, and give my mother a minimal amount of time to make the arrangements for this wretched wed—'' She blushed suddenly, realising her words were none too flattering.

''I didn't realise you considered our wedding a disagreeable obligation,'' Juan replied stiffly, slipping his clubs back into his golf bag and preparing to walk to the bunker where his ball was lodged.

''That wasn't what I meant,'' Leticia countered, her face flushed. ''It's just that Mother expects me to be interested in every tiny detail. I'm afraid I'm just not that kind of person, Juan. Of course I'm looking forward to our wedding.''

''Good, because I was about to suggest we bring the date forward,'' he said, eyeing her closely. When she paled visibly he experienced a rush of irritation.

''Advance the date? But—''

''Is the thought of being married to me so very terrible, Leticia? If that is the case, then now is the time to speak up.'' He leaned against the golf cart and eyed her carefully.

''No. Of course not.'' She laughed off his words with a wave of her hand. ''That's ridiculous. It's just getting everything planned. I'm afraid I'm not as good at social organisation as I am at legal briefs. But,'' she said with a bright smile, ''you're right. I need to become more interested in such matters. After all, we will be leading an intense social life. Your business commitments require it.''

''Only if you want to,'' he said slowly, ignoring the wave of disappointment that swept over him. He'd given her an opportunity to get out of marrying him. She hadn't taken it. Smothering a sigh, Juan made light of the situation. ''Come on, Letti. Let's go and find out what happened to that damn ball of mine. The sooner you marry me, the better. Right now my life is all over the place.''

''Is it?'' Leticia raised a brow and her intelligent eyes scanned his face. But she said no more, merely accompanied him to the bunker. Both laughed out loud when they realised the ball was stuck on a slope in the sand.

''I don't know why Juan is absent so much these days,'' the Condessa said with a sigh several days later as she and Georgiana drank coffee in the small salon. ''When I quiz him about it, he says he has so much work that he stays until late in the office. But I wonder. I would hate to think he was conducting an affair at this stage, so close to the wedding—'' She cut herself off, realising who she was talking to. ''But let's forget Juan. Leticia is dropping by in about ten minutes to bring me a list of the wedding guests. I need to get our side of the family sorted out so that she can send out the invitations. Juan mentioned advancing the date, but I think Letti is wise to stick to what was planned. May is a lovely month in which to be wed, don't you think?''

''Yes. I suppose it is,'' Georgiana murmured dully, finishing her coffee in one gulp. ''I'd better be off,'' she said suddenly, ''I forgot I have a lecture this afternoon.''

''But won't you wait and see Leticia? She'll be most disappointed. She mentioned to me only the other day how charming she found you. In fact—'' the Condessa leaned forward and her expression turned confidential ''—I think she plans to ask you to be one of her bridesmaids.''

''Oh, no!'' Despite every attempt to stay calm Georgiana paled and sat down again with a thud. This was turning into a cruel farce.

''I think you should stay and receive her,'' the Condessa remarked. ''It's probably too late for your lecture anyway.''

Realising there was no escape, Georgiana smiled weakly and agreed. Five minutes later the doorbell rang and her pulse quickened. How could she face Leticia, knowing that she'd spent the most glorious moments of her life in the woman's future husband's arms? It didn't bear thinking of.

Seconds later Leticia entered the room.

"Hola, Tia," she said, kissing the Condessa on both cheeks. "And Georgiana. What a delightful surprise. How lovely to find you here. I've a question to ask you." Georgiana smiled nervously as Leticia sat down next to her on the couch, all natural friendliness. "I would like to know if you would do me the honour of being one of my bridesmaids," she said, smiling.

"That's very k-kind of you," Georgiana stammered, "but don't you want to keep it in your family?"

"Not at all. It would be a pleasure to have you. After all, Juan has very few young cousins, and you were his mother's goddaughter. I'm sure nothing could be more suitable. Don't you agree, *Tia*?" She turned to the Condessa for approval.

"But of course you must take part in the bridal party," the Condessa agreed complicitly. "Just think how beautiful she'll look, Letti. Have you decided on the colour of the bridesmaids' dresses yet, *querida*?"

"Mama thinks we should do a replica of Velazquez's painting *Las Meninas*—which, as you know, hangs in the Prado."

"But what a brilliant idea. I can see your mother plans to make it the wedding of the year," the Condessa added, flicking her bejewelled fingers over the waves of silver hair. "I can't tell you how pleased we all are that you and Juan are about to wed."

"Thank you," Leticia murmured. "So I can count on you?" she enquired, turning to Georgiana.

"I—yes, of course. It would be a pleasure," Georgiana murmured, smothering a sigh and hoping the flush she sensed mounting in her cheeks wasn't as obvious as it felt.

There was simply no getting out of it.

CHAPTER SIX

AFTER several unsuccessful attempts at trying to persuade her mother that she simply must move out of Juan's apartment, Georgiana gave up. But knowing that Juan might walk through the door at any moment, that she might be obliged to see him and have to pretend complete disregard for the man she was fast believing she'd fallen in love with, left her restless and nervous. She ate little and lost weight. This did not go unnoticed by the Condessa.

"Georgiana, what is wrong? You look thin and peaky, my dear. Is something the matter?"

"No, nothing at all," she answered quickly, hastily buttering a piece of toast she had no desire to eat.

"Then you are studying too hard."

"I assure you, Condessa, I'm fine," Georgiana said quickly. Then to her horror the door opened and Juan walked in.

He wore grey trousers, a well-cut blazer, a white shirt and an aqua Hermès tie. Georgiana's fingers trembled and some coffee spilled in her saucer. Mercifully the Condessa was too busy greeting her relative to notice. Georgiana's eyes flew to Fernando, standing near the door, praying he hadn't picked up the tell-tale signs. But as usual the butler looked blank. She sighed, wished her heart would stop beating so fast, and prepared to greet Juan in a conventional manner.

"Hello, Georgiana," he murmured. "Everything going all right?"

"Fine, thank you," she said brightly.

"Good. I'm afraid I can't stay long, *Tia*. I have to be at a meeting in under an hour."

"Always on the run," the Condessa sighed, leaning back in the dining room chair. "Let us hope that once you have children of your own you'll calm down and give sufficient attention to your family."

Georgiana swallowed twice. She noted a dull flush rising above the pristine white of Juan's collar. For a moment their eyes met.

She couldn't bear it. His eyes, so bright and dark, immediately brought back images of their encounter in the study. She stared at her plate and wished time would go by as quickly as possible. Couldn't he have chosen to visit the house when he knew she wouldn't be in?

Then, to her horror, he turned towards her. "Georgiana, I have something I need to speak to you about in private," he said, his voice turning severe, as though he planned to reprimand her.

"I can't think what we could have to talk about that can't be said before the Condessa," she countered quickly, determined not to be alone with him ever again, unsure of the extent of her will-power should he— She stifled the thought and stared up at him belligerently.

"That," he said in a measured tone, "is for me to decide."

"Really? Well, I have nothing to say to you—now or ever." Her chair scraped the parquet floor as she rose abruptly.

"But, Georgiana," the Condessa murmured, "surely you can spare Juan a few moments?" She frowned. "After all, he is your host."

Grudgingly Georgiana realised she was not going to be let off the hook. A blush reached her cheeks. ''Very well,'' she muttered in a tight voice. ''But I have to be at the university in an hour.''

''That is not a problem. I will drop you off there myself.''

''But Jacobo is waiting. He—''

''I have already dismissed him.'' Juan's tone was autocratic. It was obvious he wouldn't take no for an answer. ''If you will be so kind?'' He opened the door and ushered her out.

Georgiana walked across the hall. She felt like a young queen going to her execution. What could Juan possibly want to say that could not be said in public? Surely he must realise that the less time they spent in each other's company the better it would be for both of them.

Or perhaps that was where she'd got it wrong.

All at once Georgiana stopped and spun round, eyes narrowed. Was it possible that for him she'd just been an amusement? That he'd found it titillating to be the first man to touch her intimately, to bring her to orgasm? A raw, angry rage stirred and she marched into the study fuming.

''How dare you?'' she spat as soon as the door was closed. ''How dare you?''

''How dare I what?'' he asked haughtily.

''Call me in here as if—as if—''

''As if nothing had happened between us?'' he asked, leaning lazily on the back of the couch, watching as her breasts heaved with restrained anger. God, she was so tempting, so desirable.

Quenching the immediate desire that surged the instant he set eyes on her, Juan looked her over.

''I hear you are going to be a bridesmaid at my wedding.''

"By no choice of mine," she hissed, turning her back on him and staring out of the window.

"Georgiana, I wanted to talk to you to see if we could come to some reasonable arrangement."

She whirled round. "What did you say?"

"A reasonable arrangement. Perhaps we could contrive matters so that—"

Stepping forward, she raised her right arm in anguished fury.

Juan caught her wrist as her fingers were about to make contact with his cheek. He stood above her, eyes blazing. "What exactly did you think I was offering?" he bit out, flashing eyes locked with hers.

"I know what you want," she whispered angrily. "What men like you think you're entitled to. You want Leticia as your wife and me as your mistress."

"Is that what you think?"

"Yes. I also think you're despicable."

"Really? Let's make sure about that, shall we?"

In one swift movement he had her locked in his arms. Georgiana struggled for all she was worth. But once Juan's lips found hers that familiar tingle of heat coursed through her, and her body melted once more, and her anger fizzled out. All she could do was succumb to his will, revel in the hardness of his taut frame against hers.

Her body refused to obey her mind. She could not resist his talented tongue flicking oh, so cleverly, the touch of his fingers grazing her breast through the thin cotton of her T-shirt and bra, the feel of him against her.

She let out a gasp when Juan pressed closer, felt his hardness grinding into her pelvis, the rush of molten desire flow between her thighs. Head thrown back, Georgiana felt Juan's lips kissing her throat, descending ever further until he reached her taut nipple. Before she could stop him he'd cupped her breast, slipped up her T-shirt and bra. Now his lips, his teeth and his taunting tongue were causing havoc.

"Don't," she begged. "Please don't." But he ignored her, and, just as before, lowered her to the couch, where he plundered, unable to resist the bewitching feel of her nipples rising to his command. The desire to assuage the delicious ache that he knew was mounting between her thighs was too much to ignore.

Georgiana arched, her eyes closed. It was unbelievably magical. Nothing she had ever known could compare to the ecstasy she was experiencing. Then he moved his lips further, undid her jeans and lowered them. As she felt his tongue discovering her in ways she had not imagined existed, Georgiana stifled a cry of sheer delight. Then, still flicking his tongue on her, he brought her careering to the edge, and held his breath as she plunged headlong into a dizzy, ecstatic haze that left her limp and exhausted.

"Georgiana," Juan whispered, holding her close and brushing the strands of golden hair from her face. "My beautiful *linda* Georgiana."

All at once his words sank home and she pulled away, righting her clothes and sitting up, horrified that she'd allowed him to have his way once again—and in broad daylight. What was the matter with her? Surely she knew he was only trifling with her?

"Juan, leave me alone," she said hoarsely. "This is dreadful. It's sordid and degrading."

"You didn't appear to feel that way a few minutes ago," he pointed out, rising and straightening his clothes.

"You're right." She looked him straight in the eye. "I should never have allowed you to do what you did. After all, it's always the woman's fault, isn't it?"

The ironic twist of her lips took him by surprise, and he stepped forward, horrified. Not only was he taking shameless advantage of this girl, but he was also deforming her view of life, of men.

"I never meant to hurt you," he said in a low, tense voice, his hands clenched as he paced the room.

"Don't worry—you haven't," she threw, trying to sound nonchalant as she passed her fingers through her hair and rose. "But I think even you will agree that after this it is better I go. How can I possibly be a bridesmaid to Leticia after this? The whole notion is horrible."

"You cannot leave the house."

"Why not?"

"Because I don't want you to."

"Frankly, Juan, at this stage what you want or don't want doesn't enter the equation. We must do whatever it takes to stop this absurd set of circumstances. Or do you expect me to go on having secret trysts with you while your aunt drinks tea in the dining room?" she threw bitterly, making him realise once again how very badly he'd behaved.

"I will stay away," he said stiffly.

"You said that once before."

"This time I mean it. You will not be compromised by my presence again." With a small bow he turned on his heel and left the study, leaving Georgiana standing alone in the middle of the room seething, not knowing whether to be happy or sad.

Furious, she picked up her books from the hall and left for class. She must end this now.

On arrival in the Faculdad de Filosofia y Letras, where her course was taking place, Georgiana walked absently up the wide staircase to her classroom.

"Hey!" a voice called from above. She looked up to see Sven, a Swedish student to whom she'd talked several times during breaks. ''Hi, there,'' he called, waiting for her to climb the rest of the steps.

''Hello.''

''So, where have you been? We wanted to invite you to go away with us this weekend.''

''Oh? Who's 'us'?'' she asked, smiling. Sven was a tall and handsome young man whom all the girls on the course found devastatingly attractive. The first week she had too. Until a tall dark Spaniard had walked into her life, eclipsing every other man within miles.

''Well,'' Sven replied, in Scandinavian-accented English, ''there's Tina, Albert from Holland, Anya from Finland, me, and two other guys from Canada you haven't met yet.''

''Where were you planning to go?''

''We thought it would be fun to go down to Andalusia. We can rent a mini-van.''

''That's not a bad idea,'' Georgiana replied thoughtfully as they reached her classroom. ''In fact it would be lovely. Thanks for remembering me, Sven. Of course I'll join you.''

Satisfied that a few days in Andalusia would help her forget all that had happened between her and Juan, Georgiana entered the classroom determined to master Spanish grammar and not allow one thought of the man to cross her brain.

But that, she found, was easier said than done.

''But why should we advance the date of our wedding?'' Leticia asked, as they sat at the bar in their favourite *tasca* on the corner of Don Ramon de la Cruz and Goya, working their way through several *tapas*, consisting of calamares fritos—fried squid—*tortilla* and *chorizo*.

''Letti, it doesn't matter why,'' Juan exclaimed, exasperated at her resistance to the idea. "It'll make things much easier. It means we can go skiing on our honeymoon. We agreed that a month in the sun would drive both of us crazy with only each other for company, remember?" He took a sip of wine.

"Really? I said that?"

"Well, not in so many words," Juan remonstrated. "But I distinctly remember the conversation."

"We're certainly a romantic pair, aren't we?" she said with a sigh, looking down into her glass thoughtfully.

"Letti, what's the matter? Neither of us ever pretended this was a love match. But you know how fond of you I am." He squeezed her hand reassuringly.

"I know. I'm very fond of you too," she said, looking up, her eyes awash with sincerity. "It's just that—"

"Look, Letti, if you've any regrets, for goodness' sake say so."

She hesitated. "No, I don't have any regrets." She shook her head, looked up at him and smiled brightly. "When do you want the wedding to be held?"

"I don't suppose we could do it quietly somewhere?"

"You mean disappear and get married? I wish," she replied longingly. "But the thought of having to bear my mother's recriminations for the next few years is a bit off-putting."

"Yes. You have a point," he agreed, and they both fell silent and sipped their wine.

"You see, for her, planning this wedding is the highlight of her life. I mean you're a duke, Juan. My parents think that is marvellous. After all, my father's a mere marquis," she said, laughing. "We're going up a notch."

"Don't be ridiculous. Your family and title date back a lot further than mine."

"I was just joking. But it is a big deal in their world."

''And that's not your world?'' he asked, quizzing her.

''Of course it is. It's just that with my work I've been exposed to so many experiences, so many other stratas of society. I'm conscious of problems and situations that people like my mother don't even know exist. Or only peripherally.''

''Letti, you're a highly intelligent human being. You don't think I'd want to stand in the way of your work, do you?''

''Of course not, Juan. But the truth is,'' she said regretfully, ''I may have to consider giving much of it up.''

''Why? I'd never ask that of you.''

''I know. But, you see, being married to you is going to be a job in itself.'' She sighed, toyed with a piece of *chorizo*, then popped it in her mouth.

''That's your mother speaking, isn't it?'' he said, eyes narrowing.

''Yes. But in actual fact she's right. You're going to need a hostess to entertain—someone who can be next to you when you need her. Not a woman rushing off to advise at university sit-ins and student gatherings. I even took part in a protest the other day. Can't you just see the headlines? 'The Duquesa de la Caniza marches' et cetera, et cetera… No, Juan.'' She shook her head and smiled sadly. ''I'm afraid I have to make a choice.''

''And you don't want to make it any sooner than necessary, *sí*? Is that it?'' he asked quietly, playing with the bracelet on her right wrist.

She nodded reluctantly.

''I see.'' He withdrew his hand and pricked at a piece of omelette with a toothpick. ''Then we'll just stick to our original plan, *querida*. How about some lunch?''

CHAPTER SEVEN

IT WAS wonderful to drive out of the city.

Sitting in the back of the mini-van between Greg the Canadian and Lucy, a pretty Australian brunette, who'd decided to join them at the last minute, Georgiana stared out of the window at the flat brown countryside rolling on and on into the distance. It reminded her of Don Quixote of La Mancha and his windmills—of which, she noted as they headed south, there were a few.

The other students were in good form. Everyone was happy to be spending a long weekend away, glad to discover more of this fascinating country.

After a while Georgiana fell asleep. But her dreams were fraught with images of Juan, of his magical hands coursing over her body, awakening her senses.

All at once the mini-van jolted to a stop.

''Hey, Sleeping Beauty, wake up!'' Sven gave Georgiana an affectionate shake and she smiled sleepily. She followed the others and entered a roadside *tasca*. Outside the low whitewashed building, bottles of wine hung in straw canisters. Inside the dark beamed *tasca*, they headed to the bar. In the corner several men sat drinking wine and beer, their eyes glued to a large television set showing a soccer game. There were occasional shouts of enthusiasm and loud exchanges when the favourite team pushed ahead.

Georgiana sat next to Sven at the bar and ordered *vino con gaseosa*—a delicious combination of red wine and fizzy clear lemonade that she'd grown to like—from the portly barman poised proudly beneath an impressive array of Serrano hams hanging from the ceiling beams. They ordered some, and he sharpened a lethal-looking knife, then sliced the ham with artistic expertise.

"I'm so glad you came," Sven said, pulling his bar stool closer to hers. "I hadn't seen you for a couple of days. Everything okay? You look a bit tired. You've lost weight," he added observantly.

"Fine. Just had a bit of a cold, that's all."

"Going south will do you good," he said, his handsome broad smile lighting up his good-looking features. "Some time you must come and visit Sweden. It's also a beautiful country."

"I'm sure." How could she tell Sven that Sweden was the last thing on her mind right now? Rather, she was wondering desperately where Juan was and what he was doing. Suddenly Andalusia seemed a long way away, and she sighed.

The kids were all laughing and joking and having fun. The last thing she wanted was to be a party-pooper. But somehow it seemed dreadfully juvenile. Had she become so blasé that she couldn't appreciate her peers any longer? Damn Juan and the windows he'd opened! She was darned if she'd allow him to monopolise her existence. She'd come on this trip because of him, hadn't she? And Sven was a sweetie. Just the kind of boy she should be going out with.

Making a superhuman effort, Georgiana concentrated on her surroundings and told herself to jolly well forget the Duque de la Caniza and enjoy herself.

That was what she'd come for, wasn't it?

As he strolled through the orange groves of his *finca* near Seville, where he'd come to attend to some pending business, Juan found it hard to get two things out of his mind. The first was Georgiana, whom he'd vowed never to touch again. The second was his conversation with Leticia, which had left him in a sober frame of mind.

When he'd thought of their marriage he'd only ever considered what it would be like for him: a convenient way of sorting out a problem. Now, for the first time, he was struck by what Leticia might be forced to give up. Another woman might not have considered it a sacrifice, would have considered becoming a duchess sufficient compensation for anything she might be leaving behind. But not Leticia. She loved her work, believed in the causes she espoused, and was the bulwark of the group of activist lawyers who often took risks and put their names on the line to speak up for what they believed in.

Snapping his fingers at the two pointers snuffling at his heels, Juan walked further into the grove. He loved this family home. The beautiful seventeenth-century farmhouse that had been in his mother's family for generations was so different from his paternal family seat in Navarra, the rugged mountainous region near the French border from where his ancestors hailed. This house reminded him of his mother, of his childhood, of hot summers riding wonderful horses, some of which he still kept down at the stables.

His mother had loved the place, and had spent her declining years here. He'd only returned briefly since her death last year, but now he felt the need for solitude, for the peace the place afforded him. It was the one spot he could truly think.

It was late afternoon when he walked back to the house, dogs in tow, and entered the cool flagstoned hall. The furnishings in the farm were of dark jacaranda—Spanish antiques as old as the house. His mother had made considerable improvements to the place, but essentially it had remained the same for several generations. Realising that the staff all had the day off to attend a *fiesta* in the local village, Juan decided to shower, then head to town for a bite to eat.

Half an hour later, hair damp and sleek from his shower, he donned a pair of old jeans and a white shirt, and looped a navy sweater over his shoulders. Soon his Ferrari was racing down the beaten-earth road, through the orange groves, leaving a trail of dust in its wake. Then he got on the highway and headed towards Seville.

He was five miles out of town when all of a sudden his eye caught a group of young people entering a mini-van outside a roadside restaurant. He did a double take and nearly crashed as he slammed on the brakes. Was he seeing straight? Surely that could not be Georgiana climbing into the van, helped by a tall, handsome, blond Viking?

Staying in the slow lane, Juan allowed the mini-van to overtake him. A flash of Georgiana's lovely face in one of the rear windows of the van confirmed his doubts.

Juan let out an oath, then carefully trailed the mini-van into the centre of Seville, circling behind it as it sought a parking spot in the busy city centre, his temper frayed. What the hell was she doing here? His aunt hadn't mentioned her going on any trip when they'd last spoken. But then he hadn't mentioned Georgiana to his aunt either.

Finally the mini-van eased into a tight parking spot and he watched, eyes narrowed, as the young people alighted. His fist clenched when he saw the tall blond Scandinavian god slip his arm possessively through Georgiana's. Damn nerve, he reflected, seething, inching into a free space only two cars down. Ramming the Ferrari to a halt, Juan got out, determined not to lose sight of the group.

Following at a safe distance, he watched the merry party make its way down a narrow cobbled street. Georgiana was laughing, obviously enjoying herself. Instead of being glad, as he should have been, Juan experienced a rush of searing jealousy. What right had she to be running around a foreign city—his city—with some man she barely knew? It was outrageous.

It did not occur to him that his own behaviour might be considered several degrees less palatable.

As they rounded a corner Georgiana turned around, as though sensing she was being followed. Juan stepped quickly into the shadow of an ancient doorway, casting a quick look down at an old crone in a long red and white polka-dotted flamenco dress and silk shawl, huddled on the step. She lifted a wizened brown olive of a face and stretched out her hand. *"Por favor, señor, ayudame."*

Keeping one eye on Georgiana and the other on the old gypsy, Juan slipped his hand in his pocket and pulled out some loose change, which he deposited in the woman's shrivelled palm.

"Espera!" she said, clutching his sleeve when he moved to leave.

"What is it?" he asked, exasperated. "I've given you all the money I can spare."

"I don't want more money. *Churumbel!*" she said, using the gypsy term for "give me your hand".

There was too much of the Andalusian in him to refuse. Reluctantly Juan stretched out his right palm, felt the old woman take it in his and study it. He waited impatiently, still able to see the back of Georgiana and the Nordic giant's blond head bobbing among the tourists and locals as they made their way down the street.

"Tell me," he said impatiently, "what is it you see, *gitana*? I have to go. I have an important appointment."

"I know you do. With destiny." The old woman cackled and shook her scarved, gold-coined head. "A destiny that you never expected,'' she muttered knowingly. ''You have seduced a young virgin, or are about to. Beware, you of the noble name, for where the flesh travels the heart may well follow.''

Juan stared down at her, taken aback.

''Ah, but you're a fine one, aren't you?'' she exclaimed with a toothless smile, squinting at his palm. ''What of the other one? The one who waits but who is unsure of her heart? Will you marry her even though you know she doesn't love you? Or will you follow your soul and listen to its pleadings?''

''You talk rubbish, *gitana*,'' he snapped, withdrawing his hand from hers. Quickly he pressed another note into her palm and went on his way. He could still just see the bobbing heads, fast disappearing in the distance.

''Remember what I told you,'' the old gypsy called after him. ''You've some surprises ahead of you.''

Paying no heed to her, Juan pushed his way forward, nearly toppling two French tourists who sent him filthy looks and muttered. Just then he caught sight of Georgiana's group, turning right into another street. He had no idea what he planned to do, but the thought of her experimenting with what she'd learned in his arms with another man had him swearing under his breath once more. His reason told him he had no right. But instinct said she was his.

For as long as he chose.

With this thought uppermost in his mind, Juan turned the corner and settled on a course of action.

CHAPTER EIGHT

GEORGIANA peered at the exquisite Andalusian pottery in a tiny shop window. Perhaps she should buy a souvenir for her mother, she reflected, noting this particular establishment seemed less blatantly touristy and more genuine than most of the others. She was about to go inside when all at once a hand clamped down on her right shoulder.

She spun round, an exclamation on her lips.

Recognising her assailant, she felt the words die on her lips.

"So! We meet again," Juan said, his dark eyes flashing angrily, his hand still gripping her shoulder.

"Wh-what are you doing here?" she asked when she was finally able to speak.

"Don't you think it is I who should be asking that same question?" he retorted arrogantly.

"I don't see why," she said, regaining her poise. "And would you mind not manhandling me?" She shook him off.

Reluctantly Juan removed his hand from her shoulder and they faced one another. "It is dangerous for a young woman to travel alone in Andalusia," he said bitingly.

"I didn't come here alone," she threw back, her green eyes flecked with gold, her lips set in a firm, unyielding line.

"No? Who are your companions, may I ask?"

"None of your damn business," she spat.

"No?" He took a menacing step towards her.

"Hey." A voice behind him made him turn to see the young Swede approaching. "Is something the matter, Georgiana? Are you okay?" He looked uncertainly from one to the other.

Embarrassed, Georgiana smiled perfunctorily. "Yes, fine. Sven, let me introduce you to Juan Monsanto, my godmother's son. Juan, this is Sven. He and I are travelling around with a group of fellow students for a few days, getting to know Andalusia."

The two men nodded, warily summing one another up like two suspicious dogs. If she hadn't been so annoyed Georgiana would have laughed.

"Well," she said brightly, "it's been nice seeing you again, Juan, but I think I should go and join the others."

"Wait a minute," Juan countered, determined not to let her go but aware that he couldn't make a scene in public. "How about dining with me later this evening? I would like to show you my mother's favourite restaurant," he said, playing on her sentiments, knowing that Georgiana would want to tell her own mother that she'd visited a haunt which Lady Cavendish would know well from the old days. "Please?" he said, changing his tone.

It was the smile that did it.

How could he transform into another being in a matter of instants? she wondered, wishing she could refuse, knowing she would accept.

"All right," she murmured at last.

"Tell me where you're staying and I'll pick you up. In fact," he said, turning to Sven and smiling as a sudden brainwave hit him, "why don't you all come out to my *finca* tomorrow? It's a typical Andalusian farm. You'd enjoy it."

"That's very kind." Sven looked uncertainly at Georgiana. "But we wouldn't like to inconvenience you."

"No inconvenience at all," Juan answered easily. "It would be my pleasure. You can ride my horses and we'll have a barbecue—or, better still," he said, improvising, "a real Andalusian *paella*. In fact, if I might suggest," he continued, slipping his arm around Georgiana's shoulder in a friendly manner and taking the reins, "why don't you come and stay after dinner, Georgiana? And your friends could join you in the morning. That way we can prepare properly for their visit. I'm slightly short-staffed at the moment," he added apologetically.

Georgiana sighed, knowing she was outclassed. Juan knew the rules of this game too well. She shouldn't go, of course, but the look in his eyes, the way his hand rested on her shoulder and the scent of his cologne wafting towards her swayed her decision. It would, she justified, be an extraordinary opportunity for her companions to see a true Andalusian *finca*. She knew from her mother that the place was spectacular. Surely it would be wrong not to offer them the chance of a visit? And if he was short-staffed—well, she supposed it was only right that she should pitch in and give him a hand.

"Okay," she said finally. "My things are in the minivan. Sven, would you mind if we went to pick them up?"

"No, that's fine," Sven said good-naturedly, and they walked back up the street. Soon they reached the vehicle and, retrieving her backpack, he handed it to Juan.

"Thanks again for the invitation." Sven shook the other man's hand and smiled.

"My pleasure," Juan answered politely. "We'll look forward to receiving you tomorrow. Take down my number and I'll explain exactly how to get there."

Sven carefully punched Juan's number into his cellphone, after which they parted ways.

Any regrets Georgiana had initially experienced as she sat in the front seat of Juan's Ferrari were entirely forgotten the instant she set eyes on the *finca*—Tres Marias.

"It's perfectly lovely!" she exclaimed as the rambling edifice came into view, a panoply of changing hues, ancient stone walls and terracotta tiles mellowed by endless seasons of relentless Andalusian sun. Even now, in autumn, bougainvillaea and clematis crept lazily up the whitewashed walls, working their way freely over the sagging tiles and framing the long bright blue half-closed shutters.

Georgiana gasped, jumping out of the car enchanted. They had decided to come back and leave her things before heading to the restaurant. As she looked about her a middle-aged woman dressed all in black, even the scarf covering her head, appeared at the arched front door.

"Don Juan—I thought you were dining in town," she said, rubbing her hands on her apron.

"Don't worry, Conchita, we are. Aren't you going to the *fiesta*?"

"*Fiesta* indeed," she muttered, shaking her head. "I'm too old to be gallivanting off to *fiestas*." She gave a loud sniff. "Let the young enjoy themselves." She looked at Georgiana, a questioning light entering her eyes.

"This," Juan announced, touching Georgiana's arm and leading her forward, "is the daughter of Lady Cavendish. You remember my mother's dear friend, who used to stay with her here sometimes?"

"But of course." The older woman unbent, her crinkled brown face creasing into a smile. "*Bienvenido, señorita.* Your mother was much loved by the Duquesa. So sad," she murmured, crossing herself and shaking her head before leading the way into the darkened hall. "Shall we put the *señorita* in the same room her mother used to occupy, Don Juan?"

"Yes. That would be perfect. Georgiana—Conchita will take you upstairs. Make yourself comfortable."

"Thank you." Georgiana smiled briefly.

There was nothing the least seductive in Juan's attitude, which helped leave her more at ease as she followed the housekeeper up the stairs and along the corridor to the bedroom. Her mother had often spoken about the delights of the *finca* Tres Marias, where she'd stayed several times over the years. Lady Cavendish and the Duquesa had met when they were both seventeen, at finishing school in Switzerland, and the friendship had remained over the years.

Conchita placed Georgiana's backpack on a chair. "*Necesita algo más?*" she asked, clasping her hands before her.

"No. I'm sure I have everything I need," Georgiana answered, smiling. "I shall take a quick shower, then go down and join the Duke."

"Very well, *señorita*. I shall advise His Grace."

Alone in the room, Georgiana moved to the window. She pushed open the half-closed shutters and gazed out over the orange groves, breathing in the delicious unique scent of orange blossom reaching her on the evening breeze. Sitting for a moment on the window-sill, Georgiana reflected upon her presence here at the *finca*. Was she right to have come? Should she simply have rejected Juan's offer and stayed with the others at the youth hostel in Seville?

Shrugging, she stepped back from the window. She was here now, so it was too late for conjecture. She looked about the austere yet attractive room. Its dark, heavy jacaranda furniture was from an age gone by, draped with heavy white linen and lace. A vase filled with wild flowers stood on the antique dresser, and when she opened the creaking door of the armoire her nostrils filled with the unmistakable scent of lavender.

Taking off her jeans and T-shirt, Georgiana wondered what she would wear for dinner. Her backpack contained a meagre selection of clothes, but she'd had the foresight to bring one dress. Rummaging, she pulled it out and grimaced at its rumpled state. Perhaps if she hung it up in the bathroom while she showered it would shed some of its creases. The thought of going to dine with Juan looking like a freak didn't appeal to her in the least. The only other choice was another pair of low-slung jeans and a clean T-shirt, and she had a pretty good idea what his opinion of those would be.

Taking the dress with her into the bathroom, Georgiana slipped into the shower, enjoying the warm water and relaxing her body. She let it run for a while. She must prepare herself for the evening. What would she do, she wondered suddenly, if Juan kissed her again?

Instead of disgust, the thought sent delicious shivers arrowing through her. But she banished them. This was her chance, she realised reluctantly, to put matters on a different footing. There was no way she could allow what had occurred between them before to continue. And if he didn't know any better, then she did.

Priding herself on this righteous objective, Georgiana got out of the shower and picked up one of the soft lavender-scented towels folded on top of the wooden chest, determined to make good her intent. Juan must become a friend, or return to being merely the man under whose roof she happened to be staying. She couldn't—mustn't—think of him in any other terms.

But it was hard not to dream of his lips devouring hers, of his hands—those wonderful hands—caressing her in ways too delicious to dwell upon, teaching her things she'd only read of and wondered if they really existed.

Now, she reflected ruefully, she knew they did.

The other worrying symptom was the fact that she now found her university companions nice, but uninteresting. She recalled how on the first day of class she'd looked over at Sven and thought, Hmm, very attractive. Now she didn't think anything at all. Other men had been simply eclipsed by Juan, as though he were the sun and they mere satellites. Every fleeting moment seemed filled with images of the wretched man.

She'd do better, she realised, shaking out her dress, which had improved no end thanks to the bathroom steam, to think of him walking down the aisle with Leticia instead of daydreaming fruitlessly.

Married.

Letting out a long sigh, Georgiana slipped fresh lace underwear under her dress, then brushed her long hair back and tilted her head and glanced critically in the mirror. She looked okay. The dress, a sleeveless pale blue number that defined her elegant figure, made her feel attractive and sexy. Not that this was her objective, she reminded herself hastily, and wondered if she wouldn't get cold, since the evening air had cooled considerably. Dabbing on some lip-gloss, she added a dash of mascara to her eyelashes, then made her way downstairs, set on carrying out her plan.

Juan sat on the verandah and waited impatiently for his guest to descend. Why had he done this? Why had he invited her here when he knew it was only courting further danger, encouraging an impossible situation? What would Leticia do if she knew?

Nothing, he realised, guilt engulfing him. She would think it exactly the situation he'd portrayed to the housekeeper. Georgiana was his mother's goddaughter, whom he'd happened to come across in Seville and to whom he had extended his hospitality.

He sighed. He was not proud of his behaviour. And it must be put a stop to at once. Perhaps this was his chance to change their relationship. They would talk about the situation over dinner in a rational manner, he decided. He would explain to her just how impossible it all was, and after that they would move on.

Just as he was warming to the theme Georgiana walked through the living room and stood, framed in the doorway of the verandah, sending all his good intentions tumbling headlong into the surrounding orange groves.

She was lovely—simple, perfect and lovely.

Recapturing his breath, Juan rose gallantly. "Come—sit down and have a drink. I have some champagne on ice."

"Thank you." Georgiana moved hesitantly to the furthest wicker chair and crossed her legs tidily under her while Juan poured two champagne flutes.

"*Salud,*" he said, raising his glass. "It was a lucky chance that brought us both to Seville this same weekend. I hope you will enjoy it."

"I'm sure I will. The little I've seen seems charming."

"I'm afraid this time of year does not offer as much entertainment as in the summer months. Also there are no good bullfights on."

"Oh, well. I really don't mind that." Georgiana shuddered. The thought of bulls being stabbed to death did not appeal to her. She glanced at Juan. He looked divinely handsome in his casual clothes, a sweater thrown over his shoulders. His whole demeanour was that of a man sure of his identity, enjoying a relaxing moment.

Soon Conchita appeared on the verandah with some nibbles, which she plaçed on the small glass table between them.

"You will get cold like that," the housekeeper admonished, looking disapprovingly at Georgiana's bare shoulders. "I shall get you something to wear."

Minutes later she reappeared with a silk shawl. "Wrap this around you, *señorita*. The night can be chilly."

"That's very kind," Georgiana responded, admiring the beautiful cream shawl with its colourful embroidery and fringe.

"It belonged to the Duquesa," Conchita said sadly.

"Then maybe I shouldn't be wearing it," Georgiana replied quickly.

"On the contrary." Juan smiled at her, his dark eyes filled with emotion. "My mother would have loved to see you wear it. In fact I would like you to keep it. In memory of her."

Their eyes met. Georgiana swallowed and Juan cleared his throat. There was something about the mention of the Duquesa that forged a bond. She was, after all, the reason they'd met.

Slipping the shawl about her shoulders, Georgiana smiled. "Thank you. I shall treasure it all my life. Your mother was a delightful woman. I remember her from the times she used to come to England. We used to have tea together at the Ritz."

"And I remember her telling me about the little girl, Lady Cavendish's daughter, to whom she was godmother," he replied, in a bantering tone. "I never imagined she would turn out to be so—" He was about to say beautiful but changed it instead. "So enchanting."

"Thank you," she murmured demurely.

Evening was closing in on the *finca*, the sky a dark, translucent sapphire, dotted with diamonds, the moon a perfect crescent. Chattering crickets filled the night air and whiffs of jasmine gently enveloped the verandah.

"It's so peaceful here. Do you come often?"

"Whenever I get the chance," he answered promptly. "I love this place. It's here that I recharge my batteries." He waved a hand towards the countryside. "Being in touch with nature is soothing. It was here that I came after Leono—" He cut off abruptly.

"What were you going to say?" Georgiana leaned forward, brows creased, watching Juan's well-defined profile. He'd looked suddenly very sad, and she wondered what he'd been about to say.

"Nothing. Nothing important."

"I don't believe you," she said, rising and joining him on the small cushioned parapet. "You were going to say something that mattered to you and then you thought better of it. Why?"

"Because it is part of the past, *querida*. Over. Done with." He looked down at her, his face harshly outlined in the lantern light.

Georgiana got the impression he was suppressing something important. But she held her peace even as a wave of compassion—or was it something else she could barely define?—went out to him.

"It doesn't matter," she said softly, placing her hand on his arm, feeling the tenseness of his muscles, wishing she could soothe away whatever pain he was experiencing.

Juan looked down at her hand on his arm. Again the tenderness of her gesture touched him in a way he was not used to, and the raging desire he experienced any time he was in close contact with her soared once more. But he restrained it.

"Shall we go to dinner?" he enquired, rising and clearing his throat. Anxious to create distance, he stepped away, removing her glass from her slackened grip, using it as an excuse. ''I thought we could wander around the city a bit first. As you know, we eat dinner very late here in Spain.''

''Of course,'' she responded with a dazzling smile. It was really none of her concern who or what Juan had been about to mention. Still, in a typically feminine fashion she wanted to know everything about the man, and couldn't help wishing he'd been more explicit. He was being perfectly friendly and gentlemanly now, she reflected ruefully, not knowing whether to be pleased or annoyed.

Then, just as they were about to climb into the Ferrari, she noticed it had shed all its earlier dust. In fact it glistened. She frowned. ''Did you clean the car?'' she asked, surprised, wondering when he could have had the time.

''No, Conchita's husband Gustavo did it.''

''I thought you were short-staffed,'' she retorted with a quizzically raised brow, challenging him as he was about to close her door.

''I am.'' An arrogant smile hovered in his eyes as they glistened down into hers. ''I usually have all the people who tonight are out at the *fiesta*. I'm reduced to only three or four.''

''I see,'' Georgiana replied dryly.

She made no further comment. But realised woefully that it behoved her to take extra care. Juan Monsanto, Duque de la Caniza, was quite a match for any woman. Let alone a young inexperienced one like herself, with her heart wobbling dangerously on her sleeve.

CHAPTER NINE

DINNER in a *bodega*—a one-time wine cellar—was outstanding. The staff were solicitous, from the owner to the lowliest busboy, and hovered attentively. It was clear to her that Juan was highly considered in the city. It was ''Don Juan this'' and ''Don Juan that'' all evening. And although he was by no means autocratic—he laughed and joked with the head waiter—she could tell the respect Juan inspired, and noted the underlying air of command that constituted a natural part of his being.

He had ordered their meal—a delicious array of seafood and regional dishes—and instead of feeling annoyed at him simply taking charge, Georgiana found it enjoyable. He knew exactly what wines to order, which dessert would go perfectly with the other courses, and by the time they reached coffee she was caught up in a tailspin of exotic food and amusing conversation that would have been hard to interrupt.

When a *tuna*—a group of students from the university—stopped by their table in their black capes and bright sashes, playing and singing for them on their guitars, Georgiana sighed, delighted.

''This has been a marvellous evening. Thank you, Juan,'' she said, clasping her hands on the table as the romantic ballad sung by one of the young men came to an end.

When he finished Juan handed him a banknote. ''And

by the way," he said, "you are very good. Have you considered a career in singing?"

"As a matter of fact I have," the young man responded with a wistful smile. "Unfortunately I need to study law and help provide for my family," he ended regretfully.

"I see. Well, here's my card. Give me a call. Perhaps I could help you." Dismissing him with a smile, he turned back to Georgiana.

On seeing the coat of arms and the name on the card, the young man suppressed a gasp of surprise.

"Thank you, *Excellencia*. Thank you very much. It was you who donated the music scholarships to the university, wasn't it?"

"Yes. And I have other plans that include music."

With a half-bow the young man followed his companions excitedly.

"What sort of scholarships did you endow the university with?" Georgiana asked curiously. This was a side of the man she had never heard mentioned even by the Condessa, who loved to sing her young cousin's praises.

"I decided to do it in memory of my mother. She was quite a musician, as you probably know. I felt that it was something she would approve of. She helped a lot of young people to study music who otherwise wouldn't have had the chance."

"But that's wonderful. I remember my mother telling me what a talented pianist the Duquesa was."

"Yes. Some of my early memories are of her seated at the piano playing. Though after my father died she didn't play as much. I think it reminded her of him. Now," he said, reaching over and squeezing her hand in a friendly manner that sent shudders rippling up her arm, "how about going for a walk? I want to show you the Alcazar lit up. It's spectacular."

When they reached the street Juan slipped his arm through hers, and together they walked through the ancient streets of the city, its many influences visible in the varied architecture—Christian and Moorish, old and modern, living harmoniously side by side.

Georgiana felt strangely comfortable in Juan's company. All her previous misgivings dissipated as together they roamed the city. They passed several establishments from which the sounds of flamenco music emanated. On the steps of one three *gitanas* in colourful polka-dotted dresses stood smoking and chatting, waiting for their number to be called. One of them sent Juan an appraising look and murmured something to her companion in rapid Spanish. As they passed laughter could be heard.

"What was that about?" Georgiana asked. The interchange had been too rapid and tinged with dialect for her to follow.

Juan smiled and gave her a sidelong look. "Maybe it's a good thing you still don't know too much Spanish," he murmured, eyes glistening mischievously.

"Oh?" Georgiana challenged. "Was it that bad?"

"Not at all. Very complimentary, in fact. But also rather daring."

Georgiana felt a blush rise to her cheeks. Obviously the woman had made some reference to them together. She wished she hadn't asked.

"Do you want to know what she said?" he taunted as they turned the corner back into the *plaza*, where the car was parked.

She shrugged. "I'm sure it can't have been that important."

"She said you could tell that a couple like us were very compatible in bed."

"Oh." Georgiana swallowed. Just as she'd started feeling really comfortable all the discomfort returned, as did a rush of heat, searing down, that left her undone.

''Georgiana,'' Juan said gently, ''I think we're going to have to face the fact, *querida*, that we are both deeply attracted to one another.''

''Perhaps,'' she said, turning away. ''But you're marrying another woman.''

''I know. And I'm not proud of the fact that I find you irresistible.'' He reached out, touched her cheek lightly and sighed. ''You remind me of someone,'' he said at last. ''Someone I cared for very deeply.''

''Then perhaps you're just trying to recapture the past,'' she retorted, standing stiffly, certain that if she weakened she would end up in his arms, giving way to the world of sensations he'd unlocked and which she longed to partake of once more.

She swallowed, wished she could be stronger, resist the magnetic draw this man held for her. He was out of bounds, she reminded herself. If she did sleep with him she would be taunting destiny, inviting chagrin into her life when he walked away with another woman.

''I think we should go home,'' she said at last.

''So do I. But think about it. I can't offer you marriage, Georgiana, but I can make your first adventure in love an unforgettable one.'' He opened the car door and she sat down, drained of energy.

''It's fine for you,'' she threw bitterly as he sat in the driver's seat. ''Afterwards you would just walk away and move on. But what about me?''

''It is your choice, Georgiana. If you don't want us to consummate the fire that burns between us I will respect that. I would never do anything to hurt you.''

''But you are hurting me merely by suggesting it,'' she

cried, clasping her hands in her lap, trying to curtail the rising frustration.

"I didn't mean to hurt you," he said quietly, starting the Ferrari's engine. "But, as you have reminded me several times, we are both adults and I think we both know that our desire for one another does not stem from anything trite, rather from something very special."

"Maybe," she whispered, "but what about Leticia?"

"This has nothing to do with Leticia. She is part of another area of my life," he said coldly. "Ours will be a marriage of convenience. She does not expect me to be faithful to her—now or after our marriage. As long as I do not humiliate her publicly, she will be quite content to turn a blind eye to my affairs."

"And what if *she* decides to have an affair?" Georgiana challenged him, livid at his chauvinistic attitude.

"That," Juan replied implacably, "would be an entirely different matter. Leticia will bear my children. She cannot be running around having affairs."

"But that's exactly what you are asking me to have with you, isn't it? An affair?"

"I'm afraid I can offer no more. You know that," he said sadly, taking a sidelong look at her. "That's the way the cookie crumbles sometimes, *querida*."

"I think it's preposterous—and I wish I hadn't agreed to come to your *finca*," Georgiana snapped, irritated with herself, and with the fact that she was even contemplating this man's outrageous offer.

"Why? Because you are tempted?" He raised a quizzical dark brow and his eyes bored into hers for a quick moment before he fixed them back on the road.

Georgiana didn't reply. Instead she remained in stony silence until they reached the *finca*.

"Goodnight," she said grandly, once they'd entered the

hall, "and thank you for a pleasant evening. Now, if you'll excu—"

But her words were cut off as Juan placed his hands on her shoulders and drew her to him. "Are you so sure you want to brush me off in this manner?" He gazed down into her eyes and his hands roamed down her back.

Georgiana tried to muster every spark of will-power but she knew it was useless. Sooner or later she would give in. As his lips came down on hers and his hands glided to her bottom, bringing her close up against him, she let out a tiny moan.

"You see," he murmured, lifting his lips for an instant from hers. "We both want this, need this, *mi querida*. Don't resist what is meant to be. And have no regrets. I promise to take care of you, whatever happens."

Georgiana's logical mind fought with all its might. This was rubbish. Juan was engaged to another woman. She had no right to do this either to Leticia or herself.

But in vain.

All resistance broke down when his thumb grazed her breast and she let out the sigh of delight she'd been holding back. It was impossible to resist, impossible not to submit to his touch, to his magical fingers dominating her body, his powerful arms scooping her up.

Georgiana lay quietly in his arms as Juan carried her up the ancient staircase and into his bedroom, where only the bedside lamps were lit. Then, laying her down gently on the heavy lace coverlet, he looked her over possessively.

She was beautiful, lovely and tender. For a minute memory flashed and he travelled back in time. This, he realised with a twinge of regret, was how his wedding night with Leonora should have been, had it ever taken place.

Then, banishing the past, he concentrated on the present, on slowly divesting the lovely creature with whom he was enchanted of her clothes, until she lay naked before him, her beautiful, lithe figure etched in the lamplight, her soft skin translucent and creamy, begging to be touched.

"You are so beautiful, Georgiana," he said, fingers lightly caressing her neck, down to the swell of her taut breasts. Her hair splayed like a golden fan over the pillows. He would, he vowed, as his thumb fleeted across the delicious pink peaks, teach her what love was all about. He would not rush the experience, however much his own desire burned him. He would take his time, the time needed to love her thoroughly, caress her to her core, show her what pleasure and lovemaking were all about.

Slowly he lowered his lips to her breast and his fingers roamed further. As they did so, Georgiana arched and let out a gasp. Then she murmured his name, caught on a new, passionate wave of emotion, sweeping her in a tide of soaring heat that engulfed, consumed, swamped her entire being. As his fingers sought tenderly within her, she experienced a release of molten heat, the coiling tension growing deep inside her begging to be freed.

Gently Juan stroked her, discovering each secret spot, a strange primal sensation taking hold. He was the first man to touch her, the first to discover her, to pleasure her. *Dios,* how he wished he could also be the last.

Again he taunted her breast with his teeth, laved it, then basked in the fall of the soft honeyed flow as his fingers reached for her and she arched eagerly against his hand. In a rush she came, body thrust towards him, crying his name, and he held her close until the last shudders subsided.

Only then did he undress and lie next to her on the bed.

Should he take her?

For a moment Juan hesitated, examining his conscience. He could still hold back—could still put an end to this folly.

But just as reason was about to take hold Georgiana

turned towards him, eyes glistening, and let out a tiny sigh of longing. Her breast stroked his side and he groaned. All at once her fingers trailed down his chest and he shivered. Then, to his delight, they shyly trailed lower, until she discovered him. Juan let out a stifled moan as timidly she began to caress him. Drawing her closer, he kissed her, caressed her, gasped as her touch grew more confident. They sought to pleasure one another—he with the experience of years, she with a centuries-old primal female instinct that had suddenly come alive.

But soon the moment came when he could wait no longer.

Parting her thighs, he looked deep into her eyes. "I will try not to hurt you," he whispered, lowering his lips softly to hers as carefully he entered her.

For a second he held back, looked into her eyes, caught the flash of fear followed by wonder as she experienced the new feel of him entering her. Then, as naturally as if they'd been making love for years, she arched, moving her hips, her body begging for fulfilment.

Juan could stand it no more.

In one swift movement he thrust and made her his, heard her stifled gasp, felt her body surrender to him, and knew the exquisite joy of possessing her heart and soul.

Georgiana let out a tiny cry of wonder and pain as he discovered her. Then just as quickly gave way to the wonderful mysterious rhythm of their bodies entwining as one, felt the delicious pain and joy of being possessed by a man she—

Loved.

They climaxed in a glorious coming together of body and soul and Georgiana knew the truth. And as she shuddered, experienced the weight of a man's body on her for the first time, she also knew that tonight she'd set herself up for a broken heart.

CHAPTER TEN

GEORGIANA blinked as a persistent ray of warm autumn sunshine peeped through the half-closed shutters. Opening her eyes, she suddenly realised where she was and turned on her side. In the shadows she saw Juan stretched out next to her, asleep, his dark hair tousled, his tanned body partially covered by the white linen sheet taking up a large portion of the bed.

The ghost of a smile hovered as she looked at him, recalling the night before, swamped by a sudden rush of tenderness. Overwhelmed, she blinked away tears. It had been so wonderful, so extraordinary, so perfect. Yet what, she wondered, as daylight poured gently into the room, awaited her now? What would the future hold? Would he want rid of her now that he had satisfied his desire for her? Would he simply banish her from his life? Or would he expect things to return to the way they had been when she'd first arrived in Spain?

Her thoughts were interrupted by the figure next to her stretching and yawning.

Juan looked up sleepily. He yawned again, and a wonderful lazy smile dawned on his tanned features. Watching him, entranced, Georgiana felt her fears subside. She would deal with those later.

"Georgiana, *mi amor*, come here," he ordered sleepily, reaching out and pulling her back into his arms.

Moments later they were kissing tenderly, their bodies

entwined, feeling the warmth of one another, caressing lazily as, half asleep, they sought each other once more. She allowed Juan to turn her firmly until she lay on her side, cuddled up in the crook of his body, his arms surrounding her, his hands caressing her breasts, while he nibbled the back of her neck.

Then to her utter surprise he entered her, slowly, tenderly, in a delicious, warm, slow movement that had her gasping, pressing herself up against him, accommodating her body to his so that he could enter her fully. Again the exquisite sensations soared, and she moaned with pleasure as expertly Juan brought her to the peak, then held her wrapped against him as though he would never let her go.

"Go back to sleep," he commanded in a whisper, stroking the hair from her face.

And, closing her eyes, she did.

"I've been thinking about what you said," Leticia murmured down the phone.

"What was that?" Juan frowned, swivelled in his office chair and handed his secretary the pile of documents he'd just signed, indicating to her to close the door.

"What you said about the wedding."

"What did I say?" Juan tried to concentrate on the conversation. He'd been having a hard time concentrating on anything since his return from Seville and the two disturbing nights spent in Georgiana's arms.

"Well," Leticia reminded him, "you said you'd like to advance the date of the wedding ceremony."

"I did?" He grimaced, remembering.

"Yes, and now I've had time to think a bit about it I've decided that you're right. It's a good idea. In fact, the sooner we get on with it the better," she said in a rush.

"I've talked to my mother, and although at first she was reticent she's agreed to start preparations immediately."

There was a moment's silence while Juan digested the information.

"Juan? Are you there?"

"Yes—yes, of course I'm here. That is—well, that's wonderful news, Letti."

"You don't sound too delighted, *querido*."

"But I am. Of course I'm delighted. I mean, it was my suggestion, wasn't it?" he said, a bitter twist to his lips.

Why on earth had he come up with the absurd notion of bringing forward the wedding? he asked himself bitterly. It seemed ridiculous now. Yet it was only a short while since he'd wanted to get married to Letti as soon as possible…to avoid the possibility of an affair with Georgiana!

"When exactly were you thinking of?" he asked finally, trying to accustom himself to the idea.

"I thought the first week in November seemed appropriate. It works well for me if it does for you. I'll have less of a workload just then. You weren't planning on a long honeymoon, were you?" Leticia asked anxiously.

"Uh, no. I wouldn't want to interrupt your working schedule," he said automatically. How could he possibly go on honeymoon with Leticia—make love to Leticia—when all the while he could think of nothing but Georgiana writhing deliciously in his arms?

Damn, damn, damn. *Dios mio*, what a mess. Surely he was too old to be getting involved in anything so tasteless and absurd?

After he'd placed the receiver back in its cradle, Juan rose impatiently and walked to the window of his large office overlooking Serrano. How could he possibly have imagined that Georgiana would get to him so much? That she would touch a part of his being he'd believed buried with Leonora those many years ago.

But she had.

And now he was going to have to deal with the consequences of his folly. He hadn't seen her since their return to Madrid—he had avoided the Castellana residence and stayed at his bachelor flat over the past few days. What was she up to? he wondered. And how was she feeling?

For a moment he thought of phoning her. Then, remembering all that rested on his shoulders, he resisted. He simply must let her go—before he messed up more than just his own life.

Georgiana sat abstractedly through her Spanish literature class and dreamed of Juan. It was impossible not to remember the magical days they'd spent together at the *finca*. Even the arrival of her classmates for their dinner of *paella* had done nothing to counter the romantic haze in which she'd floated.

Then she'd returned to Madrid, and reality had hit home.

It was over. The fantasy weekend had been nothing but that.

She and Juan had even tried to have a sensible, grown-up conversation before returning to town, with Georgiana desperately attempting to appear nonchalant and sophisticated when all she'd felt was her heart wrenching inside. Suddenly, the thought of Juan in Leticia's arms, which before then had been nothing but a remote concept, had been enough to render her breathless with agonising envy.

Worse, Leticia herself had appeared today at the Madrid apartment, and Georgiana had been forced to smile and be polite while feeling a complete hypocrite. She'd agreed to fittings for her bridesmaid's dress and listened to Leticia's plans for the wedding. The final blow had hit when Leticia had announced that, instead of taking place next spring, as initially planned, the wedding was to be next month.

Doodling on her pad, Georgiana decided to go home after this class. It was impossible to concentrate on the adventures of *Don Quixote* and *Dulcinea* when all she wanted to do was go to bed, crawl under the covers and hide from the world.

She was experiencing a plethora of new emotions so diverse she was hard put to it to keep track of them. They ranged from sexual satisfaction to shame at her own moral behaviour. Leticia's presence in the apartment had brought her situation home with a bang. Instead of the happy fulfilled woman of hours earlier, she'd felt suddenly sordid, wicked and deceitful. Now those feelings alternated every few minutes—disgust at herself countered with elation, leaving her in a state of emotional exhaustion.

Juan hadn't been near the house, which only proved that her first instinct had been right. Now that he'd satisfied his desire to go to bed with her he would avoid her like the plague and move on. Not only did Georgiana feel ashamed, she felt used—even though she recognised that she had only herself to blame. She'd been aware of the circumstances right from the start and, to give him his due, Juan had never pretended anything different. But still she resented him.

Finally the bell rang to signal the end of class and she picked up her things. Outside it was a beautiful early October day. A mild breeze blew and she swept her hair from her face. All of a sudden she saw a red Ferrari pulling up. Seconds later Juan jumped out, and, ignoring the envious looks from a group of young men who were staring at the vehicle, came immediately to her side.

"Georgiana. I've come to take you home," he said in

that familiar commanding tone that had once so annoyed her.

"You needn't bother," she said coolly. "I can find my own way."

"Well, I'm here now. You might as well take advantage of the ride," he said, opening the door, making it impossible for her to refuse without appearing churlish. Reluctantly Georgiana sat in the passenger seat, horrified to feel her hands shaking. Just the sight of Juan was enough to leave her breathless. His flashing black eyes were looking at her so arrogantly, stripping her, letting her know that he'd possessed each nook and cranny of her being. It left her devastated.

"Georgiana, we need to talk," he said, as the car swerved out of the university car park and on to the road.

"There's nothing to talk about," she said, looking stonily ahead.

"I think there is."

"Really? About your wedding, perhaps? Your fiancée was over at the apartment today. I gather the ceremony is to take place next month. You must be excited."

"Don't be sarcastic, Georgiana. It doesn't suit you."

"It may not suit me, but it expresses exactly how I feel."

"I'm sorry," he replied stiffly, changing gears.

"Are you? You could have fooled me," she threw, suddenly bitter that this man, to whom she'd given so much of herself, was about to abandon her for another woman in a question of days. "I don't know how you have the nerve to pretend to Leticia like this," she said suddenly, a knot forming in her throat. "In fact I feel sorry for her."

"We'll leave Leticia out of this, if you please."

"Oh, will we?" She whirled round, facing him now, eyes ablaze with anger. "I don't suppose she deserves anything as commonplace as a truthful explanation? Poor woman. What kind of a marriage is she getting into?''

''The kind of marriage she expects to get into,'' he replied matter-of-factly, not taking his eyes off the road while weaving his way through the afternoon traffic.

''I doubt it,'' she threw back. ''I can't believe that any woman would want to marry a man ready to subject her to the kind of humiliation you obviously have in store for her. Which reminds me of something else I have to tell you.''

''What's that?'' He stopped as they reached traffic lights and looked at her.

''I'm leaving,'' she said, her voice trembling despite every effort to contain her emotions. ''I'm going back to England.''

''That's ridiculous,'' he said harshly.

''No, it's not. I've had enough. I don't want to remain here a minute longer. In fact I'll leave tonight, if I can get a ticket.''

''You will do no such thing,'' he retorted firmly.

Then, to Georgiana's horror, the light turned green and Juan took a sharp right turn, in the opposite direction from the Avenida Castellana.

''Where are you going?'' she muttered nervously.

''You'll see.''

''Juan, I demand to be taken home immediately.''

''In due course,'' he said, ignoring her frustrated gesture.

''I want to go back now,'' she cried.

''Do you?'' Juan sent her a quick sidelong look. ''Can you look me in the eye, *querida*, and swear you don't want to be in my arms just as much as I want to be in yours?''

Their eyes met, locked, and against her will Georgiana melted. How could she pretend that she wanted to leave when the mere presence of him next to her left her filled with throbbing desire?

Without another word Juan drove on. Several minutes later they entered the chic suburb of La Moraleja, where they stopped in front of a large wrought-iron gate. Taking out an electronic remote control pad, Juan clicked it and the gates parted slowly.

"Where are we?" she asked, eyeing the well-tended flower-beds and hedges as the car moved slowly up the drive.

"This was my mother's house. I still haven't decided whether to sell it or keep it. I was thinking perhaps—" He stopped.

"You were thinking of keeping it for you and Leticia?" she asked sweetly. "For when you have a family? What a perfect setting. I can just imagine you surrounded by frolicking children. How fatherly. How sweet." Fury ripped through her again. "What a pity that it will only be a part-time job," she added scathingly. "And now that you've so kindly shown me your future residence, will you please take me home?" she said icily.

Juan stopped the car abruptly. They still hadn't reached the house, visible among the trees.

"Will you stop this ridiculous ranting?" he said finally. "Don't you understand that I *have* to marry Leticia? That I must fulfil certain duties? It has nothing to do with my feelings for you," he added, reaching across and grabbing her hands, pulling her firmly towards him. "Ah, Georgiana, *mi linda* Georgiana."

Before she could react he brought his lips firmly down on hers, pulled her roughly into his arms and kissed her as he never had before, with a harsh, determined passion that left her breathless. Uncontrollable searing heat burst through her like a bullet, lodging low in her abdomen, and that same coiling spiral of desire mounted, rising like volcanic lava, ready to erupt at his touch.

She felt his fingers seeking her breast.

She mustn't, *couldn't*, let him do this.

Yet even as her mind protested her body begged for his touch, for the delight that his fingers wrought, grazing her strained, aching nipples.

She moaned, unable to pretend any longer, and gave way, revelling in his caresses, in his hands unbuttoning her jeans, seeking further. Soon she was writhing, head thrown back in wanton abandon as expertly he pleasured each part of her. Finally Georgiana let out a small cry and collapsed in his arms.

''This is wrong—so wrong,'' she whispered, tears knotting her throat. ''This can't be right, Juan. You mustn't do this to me. Not any more. It's not fair on any of us—you, me, or Leticia.''

''I know,'' he murmured, stroking her hair, threading his fingers through the golden mass. ''But I can't help it.''

She was right, of course. He knew that he would have to respect her wish, knew that putting an end to the relationship was the only way to proceed. But still he found it impossible to let her go. Even though he hadn't assuaged his own hunger, just seeing her lying saturated and limp in his arms left him fulfilled.

The realisation shocked him, and abruptly he straightened, pulling her clothes back into place. Glancing in the rear-view mirror, he dragged his hand through his hair.

''You're right. We'd better be getting back. It's getting late.''

Georgiana rearranged her clothes silently. She felt deliciously fulfilled, yet so sad. She had no desire to speak. For she knew, deep down, that this was the last encounter she and Juan would have. She would leave later tonight. Get out before it was too late. She would invent some excuse for the Condessa and her mother. She didn't know what yet, but she'd come up with something. She had to. To stay would be to court disaster.

Three hours later Georgiana sat at Barajas airport, waiting for the London flight to be called. She had left a message for the Condessa saying that a friend of hers in England had been suddenly taken ill and that she would be in touch once she arrived home. For a moment Georgiana thought of her course, how she'd longed to come here to Madrid to study and how disastrously it was all ending. She let out a stifled sigh. It was too late for any regrets. She knew she was making the right decision.

For both of them.

Juan would realise that sooner or later, and come to terms with it. After all, he could hardly expect to have his cake and eat it. As for the wedding—she would find an excuse not to attend, and tell Leticia that she couldn't be a bridesmaid. The thought of being present while the two of them exchanged vows was too painful to even think about.

At last her flight was called and Georgiana made her way sadly to the gate with the other passengers. She hadn't told her mother of her arrival, and hoped that perhaps she'd gone to their house in the countryside. That way Georgiana could stay at the London flat in Wilton Crescent without having to give an immediate explanation for her sudden return.

As the plane took off she looked out of the window and tears caught in her throat. She'd come here so full of life and illusion. Now she was departing, and leaving behind a broken heart.

"What do you mean, 'She just disappeared'?" Juan exclaimed, marching across the living room to take the note the Condessa was extending to him. He experienced a rush of fear and anger. How dare she disappear without so much as a goodbye?

His eyes scanned the note. A friend of hers in England had become ill? What rubbish! But, knowing he could hardly take his elderly cousin into his confidence, he pretended to accept the excuse.

"I see. A friend is ill. Oh, well. She will probably return in a few days, once the friend has recovered."

"Yes. I believe that will be the case. You seem upset, Juan. Is anything wrong?" The Condessa laid a gentle hand on his arm and looked questioningly into his eyes. He hesitated a moment, wishing he could pour out his woes. Then he thought better of it, looked down at her and smiled.

"I'm fine, *Tia*."

"Good. Then I am relieved. I got the impression you were under some kind of stress. You've seemed rather worried of late." She sat down on the couch and patted it invitingly.

"Everything is perfectly all right," he said, joining her and squeezing her hand. "There's just a lot to do in the office at the moment."

"I hear from Leticia that you are bringing the date of the wedding forward," the Condessa said slowly, picking up the embroidery that was never far from her side.

"Yes. The sooner we get it over with, the better."

"That, dear Juan, is hardly a suitable attitude for a bridegroom," the Condessa murmured pointedly, looking at him from the corner of her eye.

"What I meant was, the sooner we get married, the happier both of us will be," he rectified hastily.

"Are you sure?" The Condessa looked straight at him now. "I know that your private life is none of my concern, *querido*, but as someone who holds your interests dear to heart I sometimes get the impression that you and Leticia are—I don't quite know how to put this—perhaps not as fond of one another as a couple should be."

"I'm sure Leticia and I shall do very well," Juan replied, his tone neutral.

"But that is not the same as loving one's spouse," the Condessa replied quietly. "You see, my husband and I were very much in love. It was that love that got us through the difficult times when things weren't so bright. Had there not been that love, that deep attraction for each other, I don't know how we would have fared."

Juan hesitated. His own thoughts were fraught with similar preoccupations. But it was too late to retract, even if he'd wanted to. He would never humiliate Leticia by refusing to marry her now that the date had been fixed and the arrangements for the wedding were well under way. It was unthinkable.

"You are very silent, Juan. May I ask you a question?"

"No, *Tia*. It is better that you do not." He laid his hand firmly on her arm and looked straight into her perceptive dark eyes. "All is well. Have no fear. Leticia and I will be married as planned. And I will endeavour to make her happy."

"I hope so," the old lady murmured, letting out a deep sigh. "I truly hope so."

CHAPTER ELEVEN

"BUT why this sudden return home?" Lady Cavendish said, after embracing Georgiana fondly. Her daughter looked thinner, and rather peaky, she thought. But she was too wise to ask what was wrong. That, she hoped, would reveal itself.

"I just felt homesick. I thought I'd spend a few days here, then—then go back," Georgiana lied, dropping onto the deep chintz sofa, knowing she would have to find a valid excuse not to return to Spain. But she couldn't think of one right now. She was simply too exhausted and emotionally distraught.

Why did she have to fall so deeply in love with Juan? Why couldn't she be like her friend, Emma, who had romantic adventures without ever falling head over heels as Georgiana had? What made it worse was having no one she could share her pain with, no one she could talk to about it. Her emotions were too tied up. Love, anger, pain, sorrow—so many feelings churning inside that she couldn't define. And overriding them all was the cynicism of Juan's implacable attitude. How could he live his life in this cold calculated manner? Surely he would be miserable living with one woman when he cared for another?

A sudden thought struck her, leaving her even more devastated than she already was. Perhaps it was only she who loved him, not vice versa. Maybe she was just a passing fancy in his life, a toy to be played with for a while before being set aside in favour of a more important relationship. She clenched her hands and restrained burning tears. If truth be told, she'd been a fool. A stupid idiotic little fool. A virgin whom it had amused him to seduce. And now she was paying the price for her own folly.

Georgiana sighed and tried to look cheerful, lest her mother suspect things were not right. She couldn't tell her the truth. Not now, anyway. Lady Cavendish would be so disappointed in Juan that it would likely affect the long-standing relationship the families had entertained for years. She just hoped she could keep up the façade, pretend for as long as it took to come up with a very good excuse not to return to Madrid.

"But why did she leave so suddenly?" Leticia asked nervously. The fittings for the bridesmaid dresses were the next day, and she needed Georgiana to be present. It was difficult enough to organise all these details without having absentees.

"I have no idea," Juan said, raising his hands in a gesture of defeat. "She went back to England. Apparently an old friend of hers was taken ill. I can't tell you more."

"But I must speak with her at once," Leticia said, frowning. "She must have a mobile number."

"I presume the Condessa must have it," Juan responded with a noncommittal shrug. It was bad enough knowing he was the cause of Georgiana's absence. And the truth was he must face the future.

He looked over at Leticia who, in the past days, had seemed increasingly nervous. He would almost go to the extent of saying unhappy. Was something wrong with her? He had spent so much time worrying about his own private affairs that he'd had little time to think of hers.

"Are you okay, Letti?" he asked, slipping an arm around

her shoulders. Strangely, he felt her stiffen. "Tell me—is something bothering you?"

"No, no," she answered hastily, sending him a quick nervous smile. "I'm fine. Just a bit tired, with all my work and the arrangements for the wedding. A week in the Bahamas will do me good."

"Perhaps we should make it two," he said, looking down at her. He'd never seen Letti look so concerned and so obviously worried. Surely she hadn't learned about the episode with Georgiana?

For a moment he frowned. No. She couldn't have. He'd told her about Georgiana coming to stay in Seville, and that her friends had been invited for *paella*; she hadn't blinked an eye.

Juan dropped his arm and went over to the window. He had never in the course of his thirty-year existence felt so utterly conflicted. Up until now he'd made his choices freely. And since Leonora had died he had indulged in sophisticated relationships that demanded no ties and from which he could walk away with no damage done.

But Georgiana was different.

He was well aware of the damage he'd done, and he regretted it. Not the actual moments they'd spent together—those he would never regret or forget, for they had awoken a part of him that for too long had lain dormant. But the pain Georgiana must certainly be experiencing and which he could do nothing to alleviate. That he could not forgive himself easily. How could he have allowed his selfish desires to overcome his sense of chivalry?

"Juan, you asked me if something is wrong," Leticia said from across the room, reminding him that she was still there. "But the impression I get is that maybe you're the one with a problem?"

He spun around and faced her, tempted for a crazy moment to tell her the truth. Then common sense prevailed and he smiled. "Of course nothing is wrong, Letti. Perhaps we are both having prenuptial qualms. I believe it is quite usual." He grinned beguilingly at her. "Now, how about dinner tonight? We could even fit in a movie if you like?"

"Uh, I'm afraid I can't," she said with a regretful smile. "You see, Pablito Sanchez promised he would look over all the briefs I have for tomorrow's court cases with me. Then there's the—"

"Don't tell me. I know," he interrupted with a brief smile. "You have masses of work to do and Pablito Sanchez is the one who will be taking time out from his university job to help you out when we go away on our honeymoon. He is very helpful, apparently."

"Yes, he is. I don't know what I'd do without him."

Juan looked at her and frowned, but said nothing.

"Very well, then we shall leave the movies for another evening."

"But I still don't know what to do about Georgiana," Leticia murmured, perplexed. "You don't think she's backing out, do you? It would make the wedding party all wrong."

"I have no idea. As you said, you had better phone her and find out," he said, his tone indifferent.

"Very well. I shall get her number from the Condessa and call."

"Georgiana? No, I'm afraid she's not in," Lady Cavendish replied. "Who would like to speak to her?"

"This is Leticia, Juan Monsanto's fiancée."

"Oh, hello. How nice to speak to you. I received your kind invitation yesterday."

"And that is why I am calling. As I'm sure you know, Georgiana is going to be a bridesmaid."

"Georgiana? A bridesmaid? But how extraordinary. She never mentioned it."

"No? Well, it's rather difficult, you see, because of the dress fittings. I wonder when she is returning to Madrid?"

"I imagine in the next few days. But I shall tell her to call you, Leticia, as soon as she gets in."

"Thank you, Lady Cavendish. I would appreciate it. Juan sends his best."

"Thank you. I look forward to seeing you both in Madrid."

Lady Cavendish laid the phone handset down pensively. It was almost two weeks since Georgiana had returned to London and she showed no signs of wanting to go back to Spain. In fact every time she mentioned the matter her daughter came up with increasingly pathetic excuses not to return. What had happened, she wondered, to make her child run away? And why wasn't she confiding in her?

Lady Cavendish had been forty-five when she'd had Georgiana, making her an elderly parent, but she prided herself on the close relationship she and her daughter had always maintained. Now she frowned. Like it or not, she must sit Georgiana down as soon as she came in and find out what exactly was going on. This could not be allowed to fester any longer.

Clutching the envelope given to her by the doctor, Georgiana hurried out of the Harley Street clinic and hailed the first free taxi. Giving her home address in Wilton Crescent, she collapsed on the back seat of the cab and closed her eyes.

Pregnant.

She should have guessed when she'd begun to feel dizzy. This nightmare, she realised, had only just begun. How could this have happened? They had made love only during those two days together. But of course, as it had been so unexpected, she'd taken no precautions. And now she was pregnant with Juan's baby.

A sob rushed to her throat. If only things had been different she would be thrilled at the news. But the thought of Juan's child inside her made her tremble. What was she going to do?

A plethora of turbulent thoughts and emotions swept over her as she absorbed the news and wondered what on earth the future held.

She couldn't possibly tell her mother.

Nor could she tell Juan.

Upon her arrival at Wilton Crescent, Georgiana's mother was waiting in the drawing room. Trying to appear her usual self, and straighten out her confused thoughts, Georgiana smiled and went through the motions of normal conversation. Tea was served, and automatically she sat down and accepted a cup.

"A scone, darling?" Lady Cavendish offered.

"Oh, no. I couldn't." Georgiana paled with nausea at the thought.

"Darling, are you all right?" Lady Cavendish asked. "You look rather off-colour."

"I'm fine," she lied. "Just a touch of indigestion. Must be the curry I ate at lunch."

"By the way, I got a call from Leticia this afternoon. You never told me she had invited you to be a bridesmaid?" Lady Cavendish said, raising a surprised brow.

"Didn't I? I must have forgotten. Terribly sweet of her, isn't it?" Georgiana downed some tea and tried to look relaxed.

"Very kind indeed. But Leticia seemed worried about the fittings for your bridesmaid dress. She says there is so little time. I wasn't aware they'd brought forward the wedding date. It seems rather odd. You don't think she's expecting, do you?"

Oh, God, this was all she needed. Georgiana cried inwardly, wondering how much more she would have to cope with.

"I don't think that's the reason." She glanced at her parent. "Do you think it would be terribly rude if I found an excuse not to attend the wedding?"

"What? Not attend when you've been asked to be a bridesmaid? And at this late stage? I think it would be totally unacceptable," Lady Cavendish replied, shocked. "Darling, is something wrong? If so, do tell me. Otherwise I think you must pull yourself together and return to Madrid. It would be most unfair to poor Leticia, and most bad-mannered to Juan and the Condessa to let them down at the last minute."

Overwhelmed by a dreadful sinking feeling, Georgiana sipped her tea absently and gazed out of the window at the grey sky beyond. There really was no way out. Either she told her mother the truth—and that she knew would cause the most awful rumpus—or she braved it out, faced this situation of her own making, and went through with the ordeal. There wasn't much else she could do without upsetting everybody concerned.

With a sigh, she laid her cup in the saucer. "Very well. You're right. I'll go back to Madrid in a couple of days."

"So I should hope," Lady Cavendish admonished. "You've already missed a lot of classes. I hope you can catch up."

"I will," Georgiana murmured.

But Spanish literature was the last thing on her mind right now. It was the thought of facing Juan, carrying on the pretence that was occupying her mind at every moment.

For how, she wondered, suddenly desperate, was she going to do it?

''I will pick her up at the airport,'' Juan remarked, relieved when the Condessa told him of Georgiana's imminent arrival. Too often he'd picked up the phone to call her, then thought better of it.

Now she was returning.

The knowledge that Georgiana really would be walking up the aisle as attendant to his bride-to-be had come as something of a shock. And for the first time in his life Juan felt trapped in a noose of his own making. But the thought of seeing her again sent a new and invigorating energy coursing through him, enough to wipe all else from his mind.

But she was not to be his.

Juan realised reluctantly that he'd been spoiled. He had always got exactly what he wanted. Yet now the one woman he most desired was out of reach.

It frustrated and annoyed him beyond reason. For of course there had to be a way. In fact, he realised suddenly, there was! But whether Georgiana would accept the idea or not was another question. It was one thing to marry one woman and carry on an affair with another when she too was sophisticated, perhaps married herself. Quite another to expect the same of an innocent nineteen-year-old. He did, he acknowledged unenthusiastically, have a moral responsibility towards her.

Georgiana disembarked at Barajas Airport, head in turmoil. She felt sick in the mornings, and although by midday she was usually better she still didn't feel her usual self. What was she to do? she wondered, heading towards the exit.

What could she do?

There were only two options open to her. Either keep the baby or have an abortion. And she didn't think she could face this last—didn't think she could deal with the pain and guilt of ridding herself of her baby.

Their baby.

At that moment the glass doors opened and she looked up to see Juan standing only a few feet away, a newspaper casually tucked under the arm of his navy blazer, eyes hidden behind dark sunglasses. Reality hit. For a moment Georgiana thought her legs would collapse beneath her. She slowed her pace. How could she face him now?

But before she could react he was at her side, taking her arm and her tote bag, frowning at her pale countenance.

"Are you all right, *querida*, did something go wrong in England?" he asked, concerned.

"Nothing is wrong," she snapped, wrenching her arm from his. "And I don't know why you bothered to come to the airport to pick me up. It was quite unnecessary. I can easily take a cab."

"Don't be ridiculous," he said, taken aback by her attitude. "You know how I feel about you using public transport."

"Which we both know is absurd. Plus, frankly, what you feel or don't feel is of no damned interest to me, Juan. I am not your concern," she bit back. "You'd do better to worry about your future wife."

"Why this sudden attack of aggressive childishness?" he asked haughtily.

"Oh, leave me alone," she muttered, looking away, her lips set in a tight line that boded ill.

Juan sighed. This wasn't going to be an easy task. Obviously Georgiana was hurt and angry with him. He would have to manage the situation with kid gloves.

"Come," he said, his tone appeasing, "we can't discuss

this here in the airport. I'll drive you back to the Castellana and we can discuss matters on the way."

"There's nothing to discuss," she threw, almost crying out the words. His presence, the closeness of his being, was too painful to bear. "Just leave me alone. Don't come near me. I don't want to see you. I'm here for Leticia, not for you." On that she grabbed her bag from him and ran out of the building to the front of the taxi queue, and entered the first vehicle before he could stop her.

Juan started after her, then, realising it was useless, he watched, fists clenched, as the taxi merged into early-evening traffic. With an effort he mastered his temper. This was ridiculous behaviour and he wasn't about to tolerate it! Georgiana might be young, but she had been woman enough to sleep with him. And that, he reminded himself, was what all this was about. For he had every intention, he knew suddenly, of sleeping with her again.

With quick, angry steps he returned to his Ferrari parked at the kerb and swore when he saw the parking ticket tucked under the windscreen wiper. Thrusting it into the pocket of his blazer, he got in the car and gunned the engine.

Georgiana was driving him nuts.

He wanted her, damn it! Needed her more than anything or anyone since Leonora had died. Pressing his foot down hard on the accelerator, Juan joined the traffic. He was not about to let her go just because of his marriage of convenience. There must be a solution—if only he could hit upon it.

Pressing the pedal to the floor, Juan drove back towards the city bemused. Rarely was he at a loss. But the truth was, this situation had him flummoxed. He needed to come up with a game plan that would work for all three of them.

Georgiana would have to be installed in an apartment of

her own—though actually the cover of her being at the Castellana might work too. After all, no one would suspect them of carrying on an affair. He would tell Leticia he intended them to move to La Moraleja, into his mother's house, right away. The only major hitch was getting Georgiana to agree to the scheme. Even in his more optimistic moments he had a feeling she would never be that kind of woman.

Another oath escaped him as he reached the city, and drove towards the Castellana, sure he would find her there.

Surely a man of his experience could handle such a situation? After all, he justified, he had every intention of making her happy, didn't he?

CHAPTER TWELVE

"*DONDE vamos, señorita?*" The taxi driver glanced in the rear-view mirror enquiringly.

For a moment Georgiana was at a complete loss.

Where to go and what to do? Now that she'd rid herself of Juan it was impossible to think of returning to his apartment in the Castellana. Could she go to stay with Gail, a Canadian fellow student? No, because she couldn't remember Gail's address.

All at once, seeing the taxi driver's rising impatience, Georgiana threw out an address. It was only as she leaned back in the plastic-covered seat that she acknowledged that Leticia was the last person with whom she should be taking refuge. But it was the only other place to go. Perhaps she should be truthful and tell Leticia what Juan was up to. It seemed so unfair that the other woman should be entrapped into a marriage with a man who had been so blatantly deceiving her.

And she, Georgiana, was the other guilty party, she reminded herself, cheeks flaming. The minute she placed the situation in its true context it seemed sordid. To think that she'd been a major part of it all was even more horrifying. If she had heard of anyone else involved in similar circumstances she would have been up in arms. Yet she had been a willing participant.

Had been being the operative words, she reminded herself savagely. Never again would she allow Juan into her bed.

As the taxi wove in and out of traffic Georgiana composed herself. She must come up with a valid excuse for Leticia. The more she thought about the situation the more aware she became that she had no right to hurt the woman. It occurred to her that perhaps Juan was right when he said Leticia expected him to have affairs. For, however strange that might seem to Georgiana, with her British upbringing, it was true that here in Spain things were conducted differently. She sighed and looked out at the busy street, aware suddenly that she might be doing Leticia more harm than good by blurting out the truth.

By the time the black and red-striped taxi drew up before the smart apartment building in Velazquez, where Leticia resided, she'd come up with a brilliant excuse: the bridesmaid's dress. She would justify her sudden visit by saying that she was so worried that she'd come straight from the airport to sort out the details. After all, Leticia had told her mother the dresses had already been delivered to her but needed a last fitting, so that the designer could be called immediately.

But as she stood on the pavement after paying off the cab Georgiana's confidence dwindled. She let out a deep, sad sigh and warded off the pain that threatened to engulf her once more. In a few short weeks her life had gone from the happy carefree existence of a young girl to the excruciatingly complicated existence of a woman facing one of life's hardest dilemmas.

Picking up her bag, she moved towards the front of the building and stepped inside the glass doors. A porter sat behind a desk in the beige marble entrance. Two large tropical plants flanked the chrome elevator doors.

"I would like to see Señorita de Sandoval, please," she said, plastering on a smile.

"I will call up at once," the porter replied graciously. "Whom should I announce?"

Georgiana gave her name and waited, suddenly conscious of exactly where she was and how odd it would seem to Leticia. Thanks to Juan's deviousness and her own stupidity she was about to play the most hypocritical role of her short career.

As the man smiled and led her to the lift, Georgiana felt thoroughly ashamed.

How odd that Georgiana had come directly from the airport to her apartment, Leticia thought. Then she shrugged and smiled, too used to seeing Pablito's students to be surprised by anything this generation did.

She had been looking forward to a quiet evening at home, for she needed some time to think by herself, but so be it. She'd been trying to deceive herself for a while now, but in the last few days life had become increasingly complicated. With a sigh, and determined to ignore the niggling headache that had tormented her for the past couple of days, Leticia mustered a welcoming smile and opened the front door herself, since Lola, her maid, had the night off.

But when the lift doors opened she gazed in shock at the wisp of a girl before her. Georgiana looked exhausted.

"Georgiana—*gusto en ver te*," she said, moving forward and taking her into a welcoming embrace. Then she drew back keeping her hands on the girl's shoulders, and frowned. "I know I shouldn't be asking you this, *querida*, but is something the matter? You look so pale and tired."

For an instant Georgiana was tempted to fall into Leticia's sympathetic arms and pour out the whole story. Then reason intervened just in time and she knew she had no right to confide her misery to this woman. Rallying a smile, she shook her head.

"I'm fine. Just a bit tired. Too much partying in London," she lied, following her hostess into the apartment, noting how prettily and tastefully decorated it was.

"Put your bag down there—" Leticia pointed to the hall chair "—and we'll have something to eat. Do you mind slumming it in the kitchen? It's Lola's night off and I was planning on whipping up something simple, like an omelette or a sandwich."

"Please don't feel obliged to get anything for me," Georgiana murmured uncomfortably, knowing what an intrusion this must be. She hadn't even phoned Leticia to say she was coming. Now the spontaneous idea that in the taxi had seemed so sound left her embarrassed.

"Rubbish." Leticia laughed, tweaking her brown hair behind her ears and smiling. "I gather you've come straight from the airport?" She raised a surprised brow and glanced at the bag.

"Uh, yes. Well, you see, I felt so bad about the bridesmaid's dress," Georgiana mumbled, desperately trying to mask her confusion. "You told my mother that the fittings were already delayed, so I thought it might be better if I came right away and—well, I hope I'm not disturbing you. I didn't realise it was quite so late," she continued uncomfortably; it sounded awfully lame.

"Not at all. I'm glad you did." Leticia sent her a warm smile. "You can come over any time you like. This is such fun," she said, taking Georgiana's arm and leading her to the kitchen. "After all, we haven't really had a chance to get to know one another properly, have we? When we see each other it's always with the Condessa—whom I love dearly, of course—or Juan. But now we can have a real chat."

"Yes, of course." Georgiana smiled weakly and swallowed. The last thing she wanted was a heart-to-heart chat with her hostess.

The kitchen was bright and up-to-date, with chrome and teak cupboards and a sleek bar counter creating sophisticated yet welcoming surroundings.

Leticia pointed to one of the bar chairs. "Sit down and make yourself at home and I'll see what there is in the fridge. But first, a glass of wine."

Not knowing how she could refuse the offer of alcohol, Georgiana did as she was told and watched Leticia, very much at ease in a pair of old jeans and a long jersey that looked as if it might have had several previous owners, move about the kitchen.

She seemed so different from the sophisticated woman who'd appeared on Juan's arm the night of the dinner they'd attended at the palace. Even when Leticia had come to the Castellana she'd always appeared very groomed. Yet here she looked like a university student, wandering around in socks and moccasins, her glasses perched on her head. All at once Georgiana wondered whether Juan appreciated this side of his fiancée or if he was only interested in the role she was supposed to play in his life. The thought made her blush again. It was none of her business. She must stop thinking about it.

"Right." Leticia looked over at her and laughed. "I'm a rotten cook, I'm afraid, so perhaps our best bet would be some Serrano ham sandwiches. But I'm happy to say," she added, grimacing and lifting up a bottle, "that this is an excellent bottle of Rioja that I've been keeping for a special occasion. It seems appropriate that I should share it with my future bridesmaid."

Again Georgiana's cheeks flamed, and a shudder ran through her at the thought of what poor Leticia would think if she knew the truth. She didn't want to talk to her, or share a bottle of wine. All she wanted was to disappear, have the floor gobble her up.

"That's terribly kind of you," she said weakly, a wave of dizziness gripping her. "But do you think I could have some water?"

"Of course." Leticia poured a glass of mineral water for her, then, turning, frowned. "Georgiana, are you sure you're all right? You really look awfully drained. I do wish you'd tell me if something is wrong. I promise it won't go any further." She came over to Georgiana's side and, handing her the glass, rubbed the girl's shoulder.

The kind gesture was more than Georgiana could bear. All at once the flood of tears so long contained burst forth and she let out a sob. "I'm so sorry," she muttered between sobs. "I d-didn't m-mean to, b-but—"

"Shush, *querida*, everything will be all right. Whatever it is we'll sort it out." Leticia wrapped her arms around her and soothed her while Georgiana cried harder.

Never had she felt so anguished, so guilty or so duplicitous. What a cruel joke life had played, leading her to the one person she couldn't—wouldn't—confide in. From the moment she'd set eyes on Leticia again Georgiana had known instinctively that to share her pain and remorse with her would be to destroy the other woman's happiness. And she had no right to do that. No right at all.

Then all at once, between Leticia's soothing and Georgiana's subsiding sobs, the sound of the doorbell rang.

"Damn," Leticia exclaimed, exasperated, "Who on earth can be calling at this time? I'm so sorry, *querida*, but I'm afraid I have to answer it. Please just stay here and I'll be back in a second. It's probably some wretched delivery."

Georgiana dabbed her face with the tissue that Leticia

had kindly offered her. It was now a soggy damp ball. Gulping, she stretched her stiff back and took a deep breath. She felt utterly washed out but a little calmer now that she'd had a good cry. Bracing herself, she took a gulp of water, dragged her fingers through her hair and waited for Leticia to return, determined to be brave and not cause anyone any unnecessary pain. She would deal with her problem herself, however difficult or hard it was to bear.

''*Dios mio*, what on earth are you doing here?'' Leticia exclaimed, eyeing Juan askance as he stood on the threshold.

''You don't seem too glad to see me,'' he murmured dryly.

''Well, of course I'm glad to see you,'' Leticia answered in a harassed voice. ''It's just that right now isn't the best moment.''

''I'm sorry,'' Juan said stiffly. ''Had I been aware that you were entertaining guests I would naturally not have come.''

''Oh, Juan!'' she exclaimed, maddened. ''I'm not entertaining in the real sense of the word. You only need to look at me to realise that,'' she added, pointing to her attire with a rueful smile. ''But I do have an unexpected visitor who—who is a little out of sorts.''

''Oh?'' Juan raised a brow.

Knowing very well that his macho mind had immediately assumed she had a male caller, Leticia rolled her eyes and shook her head. ''No, *querido*,'' she said in a cajoling tone. ''I am sorry to disappoint you but I have no secret lover hiding in the closet.''

''I never thought such a thing,'' he replied haughtily.

''Yeah, right.'' Leticia grinned at him, unbelieving. ''You men are all the same. Actually, it's Georgiana who has dropped in for a drink. She's a little upset, but I still haven't gathered about what."

"Georgiana?" His expression changed so radically that Leticia frowned.

"Yes, she very sweetly came here straight from the airport. She was worried about the fitting for her bridesmaid's dress and—"

"Where is she?" he snapped, entering the hall uninvited.

"Why, in the kitchen. But perhaps you'd better—"

Her words died into thin air as Juan marched across the hall and entered the kitchen.

"What in hell's name do you think you are doing here?" he muttered in a tight, low voice that left Georgiana shuddering. He sounded cold and angry, and all at once she thought her heart would burst.

"Oh, hello, Juan," she said, for Leticia's benefit. "Please don't be angry that I left that day without saying goodbye. I had some things I needed to do in London. Then Leticia called my mother and said the dress fittings were late, so I dropped by here on my way back and..." Sensing she was getting caught up in her own lie, Georgiana shrugged, managed a weak smile and turned to Leticia. "Letti, please may I have some more water?"

"Of course." Leticia went behind the counter and retrieved the bottle of mineral water from the fridge. Taking out a third glass, she poured wine for Juan while glancing from him to Georgiana. She frowned inwardly. Since Juan's unexpected entrance a strange tenseness had permeated the atmosphere.

Telling herself she must be dreaming, she turned to him and smiled. "Since you're here, *querido*, won't you join us? Then you can drive Georgiana back to the Castellana." She handed them each their glasses. "I was just telling

Georgiana that it's Lola's night off, so I'm afraid you'll have to bear with me and eat in the kitchen. Do you mind?''

''Not at all. But I don't want to interrupt your *tête-à-tête*.'' He threw a quick harsh glance at Georgiana.

''Not at all. You don't mind, do you, Georgiana?''

''Of course not,'' she acquiesced. Actually Juan's presence made matters easier. There would be no danger of having to fabricate a confidence for Leticia's benefit.

''Very well. Is there anything I can do to help?'' Juan said, throwing Georgiana a measured glance that did not escape Leticia's notice.

What was going on? she wondered, exercising her smart brain. Had she missed something? A sudden thought crossed her mind, but she banished it as quickly as it came. Impossible. Juan would never seduce a young woman living under his own roof.

Or would he?

As he settled on the bar stool next to Georgiana, Juan masked his relief at having discovered her whereabouts. He'd spent several horrifying minutes wondering where she was headed. Now at least he had her back where he could take charge. Still, she could not have chosen a more inappropriate spot to have taken refuge.

All at once he wondered what had driven him to Leticia's. It must have been a spur-of-the-moment decision. Perhaps because he considered her a good friend?

He tried to remain oblivious to Georgiana's presence next to him. But it was impossible. He felt irrefutably drawn to her, wished he could slip his arms around her and wipe away that tired, wan expression. A sudden rush of guilt overtook him as he recognised that he was probably responsible for whatever it was ailing her. What right had he to put her through so much agony when he was engaged to the woman opposite? Why, he wondered, annoyed, couldn't he feel for Leticia the passionate desire that gripped him the minute he set eyes on Georgiana? And why did life in its infinite cynicism have to play such twisted, torturous games?

It was eleven o'clock by the time they'd finished supper, and despite the initial tension Georgiana was surprised at what a pleasant time they'd ended up spending. She felt calmer and more able to face the upcoming ordeal of driving home with Juan. As they took their leave she thanked Leticia and promised to call the next day to set up a fitting with Geraldo, the dress designer, and his team.

Then she and Juan entered the lift and a tense silence descended upon them. For a moment Georgiana shifted nervously, wanting to say something—anything—to break the tension. Suddenly she decided she was too tired, and had too much to deal with, to be worried about Juan and whether he was cross or not. He would just have to bear with her as she was, silent and unforthcoming. It was bad enough that she was carrying his child and couldn't tell him.

The thought made tears rush to her eyes once more, and she turned away lest he see how distraught she'd become.

Juan watched her closely, saw the tears welling and clenched his fingers. His heart seethed with anger and frustration. If he leaned closer and wiped them from her cheeks he was aware of what was likely to follow—knew he would not resist taking her into his arms with all the inevitable consequences.

''Why are you crying?'' he said harshly as the doors of the lift opened at the garage floor.

''Why should you care?'' she replied in a tense, muffled voice.

"Because I care for what you feel," he said in a cold, haughty tone, masking his inner emotion.

"You could have fooled me," Georgiana responded, gulping a sob, trying desperately to control the tears that wouldn't stop pouring down her cheeks.

"Georgiana, stop. This is ridiculous." Juan grabbed her arm and whirled her around so that she faced him. "I refuse to let you remain in this state," he cried, his dark eyes searching her wet green ones anxiously.

"You refuse?" she repeated, shaking her head, anguished. "You, Juan—always you, you, you. Never poor Leticia upstairs, whom you're deceiving, or even me. How do you think I feel about all this? Do you think I'm proud of myself? That I feel good going behind the back of one of the kindest, nicest women I've ever met? What do you think she would say if she knew what had happened between us a month before her wedding?" she threw, glaring up at him through her tears.

Juan hesitated. "Georgiana," he murmured, his voice softening. He was unable to resist her pleading eyes, the righteous anger and the mixed emotions churning in her breast. "I don't feel proud of myself either. In fact, very much the opposite. But tell me, my little one—" his hand reached out, despite his determination to keep her at arm's length "—can you truthfully say that you regret the moments we spent in each other's arms? I know I should think it wrong. But I'm afraid I can't. But neither can I put an end to my engagement. That too would be wrong. So you see, *querida*, I'm caught *entre la cruz y la espada*—between the devil and the deep blue sea, as you would say in English. I want you. More than I've wanted anyone or anything for a very long time. I can't begin to tell you my feelings. By the same token I know I mustn't, shouldn't allow this to continue, for in the end you are the one who will get hurt.''

''I already am hurt, Juan. Far more than you will ever know,'' she said bitterly.

''*Mi niña*, you must believe me when I say that I would do anything to avoid this pain you are enduring. But there is unfortunately nothing I can do.'' He drew her close and held her in his arms, feeling her resistance wane as he stroked her back, brought her head gently onto his shoulder and held it there, soothing, wishing for the life of him that things could be otherwise.

But they weren't. And the sooner he faced this unalterable fact the better.

CHAPTER THIRTEEN

FEELING his arms around her was too much to bear, and Georgiana let out a long shaky sigh.

Sensing rather than hearing her gesture of submission, Juan raised her face and, brushing her golden mane aside, dropped a slow, tender kiss on her lips. "Come," he said softly, "we must leave now."

Gently he led her to the car, knowing she was exhausted. He would drive her home and think about where all this was leading later. Right now she needed a hot bath and some tea. He'd noticed how little she ate at Leticia's, how pinched and pale she looked, how utterly miserable. And he reproached himself for being the cause of her misery. He should have known better, controlled his emotions where Georgiana was concerned, he reflected, eyeing her wan face before backing out of the parking spot and driving up to the subterranean garage door which opened automatically.

Soon they were heading towards the Castellana.

Georgiana sat in silence, too tired to think, too unhappy to do more than lean back in the low leather seat and close her eyes. She wished that none of this had ever happened, haunted by the thought of the baby growing inside her.

When they arrived Juan did not go down to the garage but stopped in front of the building, where the night porter hastened out to greet them.

"*Buenas noches.*" Juan answered the man's greeting

briefly, before taking Georgiana's arm and walking with her across the marble hall to the lifts. "Are you all right?" he asked with concern when she nearly stumbled.

"I'm fine. Just very tired."

"Tomorrow we must talk."

"Juan, why don't we simply face it? There's nothing to talk about. You're marrying Leticia in less than two weeks. End of story."

"It isn't quite as simple as that," he muttered, pressing the lift button.

"Yes, it is," she murmured, closing her eyes, wishing he wouldn't go on making it worse. "Let's just get through the wedding, get it over with, then I can leave and you can get on with your new life."

"Do you think it is that easy?" he threw, a slash of colour heightening his cheekbones. "That I can let you go without so much as a backward glance?"

"I'm afraid you've no choice in the matter," she whispered as the elevator reached the landing and he stood aside for her to exit.

"That we shall discuss tomorrow, when you are less tired," he dismissed, slipping his key in the front door. "Right now you need to go to bed and get a good night's sleep, *querida*. After that you'll be able to think straighter."

She was too tired to argue.

What did it matter what he thought or said? He had no idea of the true consequences of their thoughtless lovemaking. Only she knew the price that would eventually have to be paid.

But then it would be too late.

He would be safely married to Leticia and whatever she decided would be nothing to do with him.

But did she have the right to make decisions regarding the baby without consulting him? she wondered, as tiredly she undressed and donned her pyjamas. Was it wrong not to tell him that she was carrying his child?

Still torturing herself for answers, Georgiana climbed into bed and turned out the bedside lamp. But sleep wouldn't come right away. It was as though her body and her mind were two separate entities that wouldn't co-ordinate. She stared out of the window at the full moon glistening through the crack in the curtains until at last her eyes closed and troubled sleep enveloped her.

In his own bedroom, several doors down, sleep eluded Juan also. As of the moment he'd set eyes on Georgiana earlier this evening he'd experienced a rush of relief that he'd found her once more. But what had shocked him was the realisation of just how worried he'd been. Yes, he'd been angry; yes, he'd been put out by her act of rebellion—but the feeling that overpowered all others and that for some inexplicable reason had led him to Leticia's unlikely door was the fear that he had lost her for ever.

Now, as he paced the bedroom, he stopped and faced the fireplace. With a frustrated movement he dragged his fingers through his hair and let out an oath. He could not let her go—couldn't bear the thought of her in another man's arms, experiencing all that she had with him.

Yet what other options were there?

All at once Juan sat down heavily in the nearest armchair. Leaning forward, he placed his elbows on his knees and racked his brain for a solution. Why couldn't he just walk away from Georgiana, as he had from all the others over the years? Surely he wasn't that smitten?

Or was he?

Minutes away, in the bookcase-lined bedroom of her flat, Leticia was dealing with her own qualms. The look on

Georgiana's face when Juan had walked into the kitchen had not escaped her. Neither had the heightened colour slashing his cheekbones gone unnoticed. Something was going on with those two. And if her suspicions were correct then she must do something about it immediately. She could not allow matters to continue in this vein, with her marriage just around the corner.

She'd thought so much over the past few hours that her mind was in a flurry. But as she undressed and prepared for bed her decision was taken.

And the sooner she got on with it the better it would be for all of them.

Next morning Georgiana felt thoroughly sick. Knowing she was too tired to get up, she sent an excuse to the Condessa with one of the maids for not appearing at breakfast. All she could think about was time—passing all too fast, narrowing her options, forcing her to take a decision which she wished she could share but knew to be hers alone.

What, she wondered, would it be like to bring up a baby all on her own? Her mother would be upset at first, but she knew that she could count on Lady Cavendish's support. But what of her own life? Was she ready at this early age to give up her youth to bringing up a baby alone? Of course lots of people did it, she argued, touching her belly, a wave of emotion sweeping over her as she thought of the tiny embryo inside, that speck of life upon whose existence she must decide.

Suddenly tears rushed down her cheeks and she turned into the pillow, stifling them. How could she ever have thought of getting rid of Juan's baby? After all, the child was all she would have left of him in a few days' time. For once the wedding had taken place there would be no more room for her in his life.

Perhaps it was for the best.

Suddenly a plan emerged in her hazed brain. And with it determination surged.

She would do it.

For him.

For her.

And for their child.

Slowly Georgiana got up, thankful she'd made it to the bathroom without being sick. Then she showered and dressed and, picking up some books, headed down the corridor to the hall. Mercifully there was no sign of either Juan or the Condessa. After telling Fernando she felt much better she let him order her a taxi to take her to the university.

Two days later Georgiana began to execute her plan. It was wrong, she knew, to make Sven a pawn in her game, but what else could she do?

Making sure it would be at a moment when she was certain Juan would be at home, Georgiana got Sven to come and pick her up at the apartment.

"I'm going out tonight," she said to the Condessa, wondering whether Juan was about. "Do I look all right?" she asked, smiling bravely. "I'm going to dinner with one of my boyfriends from school."

"How nice for you." The Condessa smiled. "Is he very handsome?" she asked with a mischievous smile.

"Very." Georgiana pretended enthusiasm she was far from feeling. "He's Swedish. Very tall and good-looking. We've been seeing each other a bit," she added, hoping that, as it nearly always had before, this information would be relayed to Juan.

At that moment the doorbell rang, and several seconds later Fernando announced that Señorita Georgiana's escort was waiting for her in the hall.

"Thank you, Fernando. And please don't wait up. I'll probably be very late."

"Very well, *señorita.*" He bowed and smiled, and she kissed the Condessa goodnight and made a good show of slipping excitedly from the room when in fact she was dreading the evening up ahead.

At least the movie would mean she wouldn't have to make conversation with poor Sven. With a sigh she entered the lift. A few evenings like this and she'd be ready to execute her plan. It wasn't great, but it was the best she could come up with.

Juan returned from an impossibly long day in the office only to learn from the Condessa that Georgiana had gone out with a handsome young man called Sven from the university.

Despite knowing that he should be pleased she was at last breaking loose from him and picking up the threads of a normal life Juan experienced nothing but hot rage. Masking it, he poured himself a stiff whisky and went to answer one of the many messages Leticia had left on his mobile.

"I'm sorry I wasn't able to get back to you. It's been an impossible day," he apologised to her, flopping in an armchair, still distracted by the thought of Georgiana out with another man.

"Juan, I need to speak to you privately."

"What about?"

"I can't talk about it over the phone."

"Is it terribly urgent?" he asked reluctantly. "I'm beat tonight, and tomorrow's shaping up as another long day; can't this wait until the weekend?"

"I don't think so. The sooner I see you, the better. But if you're too tired tonight we can find a moment tomorrow. I can come to your office, if you like. But I must speak to you."

Juan frowned. "Is something wrong, Letti?"

"Yes. No. I don't know. I just—" She stopped, then said in a rush, "There's something we need to discuss. Something that could affect our—our life together."

The frown deepened. "I see. Well, that sounds rather serious."

"It is. Which is why the sooner we discuss it the better."

"Very well. I'll ring you in the morning as soon as I know how the day looks. But, Letti?"

"Yes?"

"There's nothing that can't be sorted out, okay?"

"Okay," she answered unhappily down the line. "Goodnight."

"Goodnight, *querida*."

Juan switched off the phone and stared into space. Had she guessed about Georgiana? Was she worried for the future? What a situation: here he was, marrying a woman whose company he enjoyed as nothing but a good friend, when all the time he was crazily in love with another.

The sudden realisation made him get up and, smothering an oath, bring his hand down sharply on the back of the chair.

It was impossible.

It couldn't be.

Yet how else could he explain the myriad of feelings he experienced for Georgiana? Never since Leonora's untimely death had he felt such deep feelings for any woman.

All at once Juan recognised the blinding truth: he was in love.

And, despite this truth, it was too late for them.

Only a few more days of having to play the game, Georgiana told herself as she stood stock still while the designer's assistants pinned and measured under Geraldo's vigilant eye.

''I think we shall reach a fine result.'' Geraldo, slim and black-Lycra-clad, cast a last critical glance at his *chef d'oeuvre*. ''Ah!'' he exclaimed, twirling around. ''Here comes the bride herself. Leticia, darling,'' he said mincing in her direction, ''how gorgeous to see you.'' He wafted over to Letti, who walked in briskly as usual, her briefcase tucked under her arm, wearing one of her smart business suits and a pair of low-heeled shoes.

''*Hola*, Geraldo.'' She kissed him back, then turned towards Georgiana. ''You look perfectly lovely,'' she said, a thoughtful expression on her face. ''Really exquisite. But still a little tired,'' she said in a low aside.

Moving towards Georgiana standing uncomfortably in front of the three-way mirror, Leticia kissed her on both cheeks and placed her hands on her shoulders. She glanced back quickly, but Geraldo was moving about the studio delivering orders to his minions, who scuttled hither and thither at his command.

''Georgiana, I know this is none of my business,'' she said at last, ''but I have the feeling something is not right in your life.''

''Oh, I'm fine,'' Georgiana lied hurriedly, mustering a brave smile and trying to look relaxed.

''Are you sure?'' Leticia's piercing glance was hard to avoid. ''I get the impression that something isn't right at all. And I want you to know that *whatever* it is—'' she put emphasis on the word ''whatever'' ''—I am your friend. If you ever wish to confide in me your confidence would go no further. Remember I am a lawyer. I am used to client-attorney confidentiality.'' She smiled and squeezed Georgiana's shoulders.

"I—I'm really all right," Georgiana said, swallowing the knot forming in her throat. "Just a little tired, as you remarked."

"Very well." Leticia sighed. "I won't insist. But remember, if you need me you can call. Day or night. No problem." She removed her hands from Georgiana's shoulders and proceeded to inspect the dress. "I think it's rather a success, don't you? Though, actually, as it's white, you will look much more of a bride than I will," she said with a good-humoured laugh. "Geraldo, doesn't she look divine?"

"Gorgeous, darling—simply *divina, lindissima,*" Geraldo cooed, clasping his hands in awe and gazing lovingly at the object of his own brilliance. "I really do come up with masterpieces from time to time, don't I?" he added modestly.

Leticia and Georgiana's eyes crossed in the mirror and for a moment they were in strong danger of bursting into fits of giggles. Mercifully Geraldo hurried off, hands waving, with more orders for his troops, and the girls were able to give way to their mirth.

Georgiana sat down carefully on the edge of a spindly gold-leafed chair, trying not to crush the beautiful white chiffon creation. "I'm terrified to do anything lest I get reprimanded by the master himself," she whispered, still giggling.

"Oh, don't worry about him. He's a sweetie at heart. I just hope I won't look ridiculous." Leticia grimaced. "I made him promise to keep my dress very plain. And up till now he hasn't dared add one frill or ruffle to it. This whole wedding thing is rather silly in the first place. After all, Juan and I are far too old to be parading about in wedding garb."

"Oh, but surely you want to have a lovely wedding,"

Georgiana said, swallowing. "After all, it's a day to remember for the rest of your life." Her voice caught and she turned away to take a deep breath. The image of Juan and Leticia wreathed in smiles, walking down the aisle as a married couple, was too much to bear.

"In a way. But you see neither Juan nor I have any illusions about our marriage. It is the sensible thing to do for both of us. That's all."

Georgiana looked over at Leticia, half turned towards the window. To her surprise she caught a deep, enduring sadness in the older woman's eyes.

"But aren't you thrilled to be marrying him?"

"No, not thrilled. I am—I am fulfilling my obligations."

"But that's awful!" Georgiana exclaimed, grimacing as a pin nicked her leg.

"I know it must seem so." Leticia turned and smiled down at her. "But at my age I have no illusions left about what can and can't be. If things were different... The other day I almost said something to him, but—" She cut off, sighed, then shrugged. "But they're not. And life must go on as it always had. Juan needs an heir to keep the de la Caniza dynasty alive. I happen to be suitable wife material."

"You make it sound like a job," Georgiana said glumly, thinking how much she would give to be in Leticia's shoes, how lovely it would be if right now she was preparing to marry the man she loved. But he was destined for another.

"Well, I suppose in a way it is a job," Leticia replied, sitting down opposite her and taking her hands in hers. "Georgiana, won't you tell me what's wrong, *querida*, I hate to see you so wound up."

For a moment she was tempted to spill the beans. But she caught herself just in time. If Leticia had been anybody else, and the truth had been anything else at all, she would have poured out the whole story. Unfortunately this was the one taboo subject. She would not, could not, destroy Leticia's faith in her marriage. However weird the arrangement seemed to her personally, Georgiana recognised that she had no right to burst Leticia's bubble—even if it seemed a superficial one.

"I'm fine. Just some problems with a guy I'm in class with," she lied, knowing she had to come up with something Leticia would believe.

"I see." Leticia frowned, then her brow cleared. "Nothing too serious, I hope?"

"No. But we quarrelled. I'm seeing him tonight. I think we can sort it out."

"Good. You've taken a big weight off my mind."

And she did look relieved, Georgiana realised. Had Leticia suspected that she and Juan had something going on?

"I'd better get changed and be off to class," she murmured, smiling briefly and disappearing into the changing room. When she exited Geraldo was chattering with Leticia nineteen to the dozen, and after brief kisses and hasty goodbyes she was able to slip away.

How long was this torture going to last? she wondered, hailing a taxi. If a dress fitting was hell, imagine what the actual wedding would be like.

What a farce, she concluded angrily. What a bloody farce.

And she was the principal player in it.

CHAPTER FOURTEEN

IT WAS past ten o'clock when Juan pulled up in the garage of Leticia's building. He was tired, but since he'd promised her he would meet to talk he'd come as soon as he could. As he parked the Ferrari he noticed another car, a Seat, parked in the other visitor's parking place. He made a mental note to tell her someone was hogging the spot, then headed up in the lift.

Upon ringing the doorbell the maid, Lola, answered.

"Don Juan," she said, a shocked expression covering her face. "The *señora* wasn't expecting you."

"I know. I should have phoned. Is she in?"

"Yes. She's—she's entertaining a guest. If you'll allow me, I'll advise her of your arrival."

Juan frowned as Lola scuttled off in the direction of Leticia's study. Who on earth could Letti have over at this time—and in the study? he wondered.

"If you will come this way," Lola said when she reappeared, looking more composed and straightening the white lace apron over her black uniform.

Juan followed her to the study, surprised to see a man he'd never met before rising from the armchair near the fireplace.

"Ah, Juan." Leticia smiled nervously and came to greet him. "May I introduce Pablito Sanchez, my friend and colleague? We're working late on a project for the university."

"Pleased to meet you." Juan stretched out his hand and

the two men shook hands while summing each other up. Pablito Sanchez was not very tall, and was greying at the temples. He had a scholarly look, and wore jeans and a light blue V-neck sweater that had seen better days. He also seemed very at ease with Leticia.

Juan frowned. "I'm sorry if I've disturbed you both," he said, his tone noncommittal. "I was in the neighbourhood and thought I'd drop in," he lied.

He'd had every intention of having a long serious conversation with Leticia. A conversation *she* had solicited. That was out of the question under the present circumstances. But perhaps it was better that way. For all at once the realisation of what, in a moment of anxiety and madness, he'd thought of doing seemed utterly impossible. How could he tell this woman he didn't want to go through with a wedding only days away? How would she appear before her friends and colleagues? At this very moment Pablito was formally congratulating him on his upcoming nuptials. It was unheard-of to humiliate Leticia in such a manner.

As he sat down and accepted a glass of red wine from Letti, Juan felt as though a vice were slowly squeezing him in its grip. Each day, each hour, was a growing inferno. Knowing that he had finally found the woman he loved, and that despite those feelings was obliged to give her up in the name of duty and honour was an unbearable burden.

But bear it he would.

An hour later, after a pleasant chat, Pablito tactfully rose to take his leave. He picked up an old tweed jacket and smiled wistfully. "I'll see you tomorrow in the office, Letti. She's a great lawyer, you know—the bulwark of our organisation," he said, turning to Juan. "I hope she'll continue to be so after she's married."

The words were almost a challenge, and Juan caught the gleam in the other man's eye.

"I certainly hope that Letti won't feel in any way stunted by her marriage," Juan said, rising as the other man prepared to take his leave. "She's a free agent."

Pablito shrugged, shook his hand and smiled. "I hope so. I see too many brilliant women change the minute they're married and their obligations force them to give up something they love and that fulfils their lives."

As Leticia accompanied her guest to the front door Juan thought about Pablito's words, and what Leticia had said the other day, about probably having to give up part of her work to attend to her obligations as his wife.

He shoved his hands in his pockets. *Dios mio*, what a situation. In truth, they would both be far better off if she married someone like Pablito and he— Well, he would give anything, he acknowledged suddenly, to marry the object of his dreams. How ridiculous that all these years he'd cynically rejected love and romance, yet here he was, caught in the midst of it. Had he met Georgiana even months or weeks earlier it might have been different. Now it was too late.

For all three of them.

The big question in Georgiana's mind was how to keep pretending she was dating Sven, yet not allow the poor boy to get close to her. He'd tried to kiss her earlier, in the movies, and she'd moved away, hoping she hadn't rejected him too openly. But the thought of being kissed by any man other than Juan was repugnant to her.

Now, as they drove home and she saw Juan's Ferrari pulling up in front of them outside the building, she gritted her teeth. This was her chance to end it once and for all. To show Juan that she was otherwise occupied than thinking of him, that whatever had happened between them was finally over.

Making sure Juan was getting out of the car and could see them in the full glare of the street lamp, she mustered her courage and reached across and touched Sven's cheek.

"Thank you. It was a lovely evening."

Surprised, but taking her signal for what it was—an obvious invitation—Sven leaned over and, slipping his arms around her, took her in his arms and kissed her.

Juan's hand clenched on the car door handle. In one swift movement he slammed it shut, then watched for a few long seconds as Georgiana kissed her companion. Fury such as he had never experienced seized him. As she exited the vehicle and Sven drove off he marched towards her in a cold, blind rage.

"How dare you?" he spat, oblivious of the doorman, trying to appear discreet but taking in every word. "How dare you kiss that boy?" He grabbed her arm and frog-marched her through the lobby. "I want an explanation," he demanded, his voice quietly furious. "And you will give me one."

"I shall give you nothing of the sort," she answered, her voice trembling, her strength waning at the touch of his arm gripping hers. "I owe you no explanation whatsoever. My life is my own."

"No, it bloody well isn't. *Por dios,*" he muttered, his dark eyes flecked with such suppressed anger that Georgiana shuddered inwardly.

When they reached the apartment he unlocked the front door and held it stiffly for her. There was nobody about and he pointed to the study door. "In there," he ordered, in such a masterful tone that she hesitated to refuse. Also, she reflected, if they were going to have it out it would be better to do so in the privacy of the study rather than the drawing room, where the Condessa might suddenly appear.

"I have no reason to justify any of my behaviour to you," she said, determined to take the offensive as soon as the door closed behind him.

"That's what we shall see."

In two quick steps he marched across the room and pulled her roughly into his arms. "How dare you let any man sully your lips?" he muttered, eyes blazing. Then his mouth clamped down on hers, devouring her, as though wanting to erase all memories.

His hands coursed over her body possessively, knowingly. He pressed the small of her back, forcing her against him, obliging her to feel the power of his passion hard and throbbing against her.

And all she could do was let out a tiny cry, try to push him away, then submit to his will, her mind and her body unable to resist the onslaught.

Juan threaded the fingers of one hand through her hair, pulled her head back and surveyed her, eyes burning into hers, as the other methodically unbuttoned her blouse, letting her know there would be no escape. Next he unhooked her bra and moved her towards the couch, his eyes never leaving hers. Once she was pinned against the cushions, unable to resist him, his lips fleeted to her throat, where he planted a slow, taunting trail of kisses that descended relentlessly until he reached the swell of her breasts.

His hands were holding her hips in a firm grip and Georgiana let out a moan, her nipples taut and aching with desire, the heat within her soaring to new and unimagined heights. She almost begged him to stop playing, taunting, and finally reach them. Then suddenly his tongue flicked the pink-tipped mounds and she let out a cry as she melted, thrusting towards him in a plea for completion. Ignoring her, Juan took the tip of each breast between his lips. Slowly he played there, never giving way, feeling her rising anguish, determined to punish her for what he considered her betrayal.

Never would another man give her such pleasure, he vowed, using every art he knew to seduce her so thoroughly that she arched, moaning. His fingers reached lower, and he was satisfied when he dragged off her skirt and panties and his fingers glided inside her. She was all unfettered warmth. Wet and wanting, however much she pretended not to be.

Now she was his once more.

For all she'd kissed that boy tonight, she was his—and would be so again and again.

Leaving her just long enough to drag off his clothes, Juan gazed down at the beautiful vision before him. He'd turned on only one lamp and the soft glow bathed her creamy skin. Looking her over possessively, Juan lowered his body to hers, then in one swift, possessive thrust he entered her. Tonight he would teach her who owned her, who possessed her. To whom she belonged.

Unable to think, or do more than take him inside her, Georgiana curled her legs about Juan's waist and, arching, came to meet him thrust for thrust. This was no gentle lovemaking but a primal need for satisfaction, to possess, to know one another as never before.

When at last they climaxed it was together. A long, shuddering endless wave of joy that continued long after they lay spent among the crushed cushions, listening to the beating of each other's hearts.

Next morning Georgiana woke up surprised at how wonderfully relaxed she felt, despite the dire situation she now faced. Strangely, her anxiety was gone and she knew now what she had to do.

They hadn't talked, just lain in each other's arms, savouring one another. But one thing she was sure of: Juan loved her. He might be marrying Leticia, but he loved *her*. And that, she knew, was enough to make the decision which only days before had tormented her seem obvious: she would keep her baby.

Now, with the decision taken, she experienced a wave of calm. But she knew that it made it impossible to go through with the travesty of her being a bridesmaid at the wedding.

Once she'd risen and showered, and got past the early-morning queasiness, Georgiana carefully packed her belongings and rang her mother. She would not run away this time, but do things right. The message machine answered and she told her parent that she was coming home and had something important to tell her.

Then she sought out the Condessa.

"But why are you leaving?" she cried, horrified.

"Because I have to, Condessa. It has nothing to do with Madrid. I love it here. But unfortunately I have to leave. It is better that way."

With unusual insight the Condessa smiled at her sadly. "Sit down, Georgiana. I want to talk to you."

Georgiana sat down next to the Condessa and waited. She'd rehearsed a speech, but knew now that she could not go through with it.

"Georgiana, I will ask this of you plainly and I would like a truthful answer. Are you and Juan in love?"

Georgiana was so shocked at the suddenness of the question she almost choked.

"I was not born yesterday," the Condessa continued. "Also, I have been in love myself. I see the way his eyes follow you, the way you try to pretend indifference when he is in the room."

Georgiana took a deep breath. She glanced up and realised there was no use lying. "Yes," she said finally. "I am in love with him. Which is why I'm sure you'll understand that I must leave. It would be utterly wrong if I stayed and got in the way of him and Letti. Their wedding is but days away. I just can't do it." Her voice caught and the Condessa's hand covered hers.

"Poor child," the Condessa said sympathetically. "What a situation. If only you and he had met before."

"But we didn't," Georgiana said bitterly. "And now it's too late. He's made it very clear that the wedding must go ahead."

"Well," the Condessa pondered sadly, "it would be a scandal if the engagement were broken off at this late stage. And you're right. Poor Leticia. Though of course it wouldn't be her heart that would be broken but her pride. Which can be ten times worse."

Georgiana found it hard to understand this reasoning, but she accepted it. "I hope you will help me find a suitable excuse for not being bridesmaid at her wedding," she said at last. "You see I d-don't think I could bear seeing them—" Her voice ended in a sob and the Condessa's arms flew about her.

"Oh, you poor, poor child," the old lady repeated, devastated. "If I'd dreamed something like this could happen I never would have suggested you come and stay. But how could I guess that such a thing would occur?"

"You couldn't," Georgiana said between muffled sobs. "It is my fault for allowing him to—"

"You mean this whole thing has gone further than just an exchange of feelings?" the Condessa said, drawing back while keeping her hand on Georgiana's shoulders and surveying her closely. "So that is why you are so peaky and looking so tired. Why, Juan should be whipped for what he has done. He had no right to seduce you when he was engaged to another woman,'' she said severely.

''He didn't do it alone,'' Georgiana replied, a wavering smile hovering on her lips. ''It takes two to tango, Condessa. He did nothing that I wasn't a party to. The truth is we couldn't resist our feelings for one another. And now it is up to me to see that our relationship comes to an end.'' She turned away and wiped a tear.

''It seems too cruel,'' the older woman whispered, her hands dropping into her lap. ''But you are right, Georgiana, and very brave. This is the only solution. I shall help you carry this through, *querida*. I will talk to Leticia and create a suitable excuse. Perhaps a problem at home with which you have to help your mother. Don't worry. Letti will have so much to do she won't have time to linger too long over this. As for Juan—'' her voice turned angry ''—I shall have something to say to him when he gets back tonight.''

''Please.'' Georgiana laid a hand on the Condessa's arm. ''Don't be angry with him. It must be hard for him to do his duty. Just don't let him come after me. That's all I ask. I need time on my own to get over this. For him it will be different. Soon he'll be caught up in his new life and he'll forget all about me.''

''We shall see,'' the Condessa replied cryptically. ''But for now let us get on with seeing to your arrangements. I will tell Fernando I received a call from England and that you have to leave. That will take care of the household.''

''Thank you.'' Georgiana pressed the Condessa's hand and they exchanged a long look. She felt better now that at last she had shared part of the truth.

Now, at least, she could leave with a clean conscience.

CHAPTER FIFTEEN

"BUT, Georgiana, there is no question of your dropping out of university! You must go back to Madrid and finish your course. And as for this nonsense of refusing to be Leticia's bridesmaid—why, it's unheard of. The dresses have been fitted, the wedding party compiled. I'm very surprised that you would even think of such a thing."

"Mother, I've already explained to Letti that I can't go through with it. She understands," Georgiana said patiently, wishing the wave of nausea would pass.

"Just because you've had a tiff with some young man in your class? Really, Georgiana, I find it hard to believe that you would allow something so trivial to deter you from doing what I can only consider as your family duty."

"Mother, it wasn't trivial. It was very upsetting and I'm still not over it." Thank goodness she'd not opted to tell Lady Cavendish the truth. Yet.

"Well, I'm sorry, darling. Far be it from me to want to see you unhappy, but I do feel that a little backbone at these moments can do wonders."

"I know you do. Perhaps you're right. I think I'd like to go away, but not back to Spain. Maybe I could transfer to Paris, or Florence, or somewhere else?"

"I hardly think that running away the minute something goes wrong is the right course of action, Georgiana. You would do better to pull yourself together and get over it there."

''Well, I'm not going back and that's that,'' Georgiana muttered in a voice that sounded petty but which she couldn't alter without giving way to her feelings.

If only her mother knew what was truly going on. But how could she tell her? How could she break the news when it was still so difficult for her to assimilate? Once she was past three months, once she felt her body changing and her tummy growing, then it would be easier somehow. But right now she just couldn't face the recriminations she knew would surely accompany such a confession, and the inevitable demand to know who the father of her unborn child was.

No, Georgiana decided, watching her mother's forbidding expression, she'd find some way around the problem, but right now telling the truth just wasn't an option.

''I'm shocked and appalled,'' the Condessa said, eyeing Juan from her perch on a high-backed Queen Anne chair. ''You have seen fit to seduce a girl whom I brought into this house under our protection. I am astounded that you would behave in such a manner.''

''*Tia*, I know very well that there is no excuse,'' Juan said heavily, taking off his blazer and dropping it on the back of the chair. ''My only excuse, if you can call it one, is that I love her.''

''That's all very well.''

''I know.'' He nodded. ''I am entirely to blame for this whole lamentable episode. When she tried to put a stop to it, I insisted. I couldn't let her go, couldn't bear to think of her in another man's arms, couldn't—'' Juan cut himself off, moved towards the tray of decanters and poured himself a stiff drink. ''The truth is, *Tia*, that part of me died with Leonora. Or so I thought. That is why it wasn't a problem to agree to a marriage of convenience with Letti.

And then Georgiana came so unexpectedly into my life. It was as if a light had been switched on inside me. I couldn't help what I did. We were drawn to one another like magnets."

"I understand," the Condessa said, her voice softening as she watched him sit heavily down on the couch, his body language so different from his usual proud tall stance. "I too have been in love. In fact I am going to tell you a story."

Juan looked up and frowned, for the expression in his aunt's eyes was filled with love and understanding.

"When I first met your father's cousin I was engaged to be married to a *marques* in Navarra. Everything was arranged—the wedding, the bridal trip—*everything*. I didn't love him, but in those days one obeyed one's parents' wishes. And then Pedro came along. I'll never forget the moment we first met." The Condessa's eyes went soft and misty. "We saw each other across a room at the country residence of a friend. It was a shooting party near Toledo. You remember that lovely old song 'I took one look'? Well, that is how it was for us. I didn't care that he was an impoverished *conde* rather than the wealthy *marques* my parents had chosen for me.

"There was an awful rumpus, of course. My father threatened to cut me off without a penny. But in the end love won the day. And I loved him till the day he died. I still do." Her eyes glistened with tears. "Juan, if there is any way that you can prevent inflicting the pain that you and Letti and this poor child will all end up suffering, I counsel you to try. I know how shaming it would be for Leticia to be spurned at the last moment. But perhaps, as you're both mature people, you could find a way out?"

"Don't you think I've been beating my brains trying to find a solution, *Tia*? Believe me, there is no way," Juan said bitterly, taking a long gulp of whisky. ''I've spent the better part of the past few days wondering how it could be achieved, but I'm afraid it would be impossible. In your case it was *you*, the woman, who broke off the engagement. In mine it would be a dishonour to Leticia's name, as well as mine.''

''You are right.'' The Condessa sighed sadly. ''But nevertheless I shall say my prayers. God has a funny way of righting things when they are meant to be.'' Then she rose and, dropping a kiss on his brow, left the room.

CHAPTER SIXTEEN

"GEORGIANA has left again?" Leticia sat down on the plump brocade sofa and frowned at the Condessa. "That strikes me as very strange. A problem in the family, you say? She never mentioned anything."

"Yes—a cousin whom they are very close to."

"I see." Leticia said no more, but she had her own ideas about why Georgiana had left—ideas that confirmed her initial suspicion. She'd been fooled by the girl saying she was going out with a boy from the university. But now it all made sense and fell into place.

"I must see Juan at once," she said, getting up hastily and straightening her skirt. "Will he be home soon?"

"I'm afraid I can't tell you. He seems to be working himself to the bone these days. No doubt he's getting a lot done before leaving on your honeymoon," the Condessa countered, smiling.

"No doubt. Yes. Well." Leticia clasped her hands together, then smiled a little too brightly. "Will you please tell him that I shall be at home tonight and won't go to bed until he comes over? I have something very important I simply have to talk over with him."

"Very well, *querida*, of course I'll tell him. But are you sure it is wise?" The Condessa looked at her long and deeply.

"Oh, yes, Condessa, I'm very, very sure." Leticia

clasped her hands again, then extended them to the older woman, smiling. ''Wish me luck,'' she whispered.

Then, pressing the Condessa's hands quickly, she rushed from the room, leaving the Condessa heaving a deep sigh. What on earth was going on? Leticia was not at all herself. Also she got the impression that the news about Georgiana had very little to do with the worried expression she had read in the younger woman's eyes.

With another sigh the Condessa leaned back in the armchair. There was little she could do to help these young people. All she could do was pray that the good Lord would handle this mess in His own fashion, and that, as they sometimes did, things would turn out for the best in the long run.

Juan had not slept all night, and the day was a busy one, packed with unavoidable meetings. Several times he was tempted to call Georgiana in London, but each time he stopped himself.

She had gone. And he had no right to hold her back. She had made her choice. For him to impose his will now would be wrong. He was about to be married. And although he longed to maintain a relationship with Georgiana he knew he would be creating impossible obstacles in her life. When finally he received his secretary's message saying that Leticia expected him for dinner without fail the news just about crowned everything.

He would go, of course. She deserved this minimal courtesy. And he might as well get used to the fact that in less than ten days his life would change radically. The least he could do was give Leticia the respect she was owed as his fiancée.

At nine-thirty Juan rang Leticia's doorbell and waited impatiently for someone to answer.

"Good evening," he said, and dropped a kiss on her cheek, surprised that she'd answered the door herself. "Where's Lola? Out on the tiles again?"

"I gave her the evening off."

"I see." He took a quick look around but she was obviously alone.

"Why don't you come in and have a drink?" Leticia said with an over-bright smile. She seemed strangely nervous, and Juan gave an inner sigh. What else lay in store for him this evening? he wondered. He sensed something was wrong and that she wanted to talk. But what about?

"I'll have a whisky," he said, following her into the pleasant open living room and dropping onto one of the wide contemporary-styled sofas, too weary to really care.

"Juan, I know you probably think it odd that I asked you here tonight," Leticia said, glancing at him as she poured whisky into an ice-filled glass, "but I—I need to—to tell you something."

Juan looked up, read the anxiety in her eyes, and his heart softened. Poor Letti. He'd never bothered overmuch about her feelings, or how she felt. She always came over as so strong and capable and cheerful. It had never crossed his mind that she too might have worries of her own to deal with. When she handed him the drink he pulled her down next to him on the sofa and smiled at her.

"I'm afraid you have a very selfish future husband," he said wryly. "Please forgive me. Lately I've been rather preoccupied with one thing and another. Tell me, *querida*, how can I help you?"

"Well, that's the thing," she said, clasping her hands and shifting on the cushions in a nervous manner. "You can't. You see, something has happened, Juan—something I feel that it's only fair to tell you— What I mean is— Oh, this is coming out so badly!" she exclaimed, rising, hands clasped, sudden tears making her eyes glisten and her words incoherent.

Juan frowned and looked at her amazed, unaccustomed to seeing her anything but in full control. "Leticia, what on earth is the matter?" he asked, getting up and slipping an arm around her. It was most unusual, in fact unheard of, to see her in such a nervous state.

"I'm sorry, Juan." She shook her head sadly and moved away. "You must think me a complete idiot. And I suppose I am. But, believe me, I rarely get into a tizzy about anything. It's just that—"

"Just that what?" he prompted, seating her down next to him again, aware that she was truly distressed and grasping her hand in his.

"Well, you see, I haven't been entirely frank with you." Colour slashed her cheeks and her eyes avoided his.

"What do you mean?"

"I mean that—well—I—to tell you the truth, there's someone in my life," she said in a rush. "I meant to tell you, have wanted to, but it didn't seem relevant because I never let it go any further than friendship. But then the other day—*Ay dios mio.*"

Leticia clutched her handkerchief to her lips and turned away, more tears welling in her eyes.

"I couldn't help myself, Juan. I never realised that I loved him, never admitted it to myself, and now it's too late. I'm so sorry. It won't affect our arrangement in any way, I assure you, but I didn't feel I could marry you without you knowing why—well, if I'm not—you know—very forthcoming at first—you know what I mean..." Her voice trailed off and her head drooped in blushing embarrassment.

"Letti, hold it a minute and let me get this straight," Juan commanded, trying for the life of him to understand this garbled admission of guilt. "What exactly has happened? Please speak plainly, my dear. It's too important for both of us. Are you really in love with someone else?"

The thought sent his heart soaring.

Then it plummeted once more.

For what would it change? He doubted there was time to cancel the much-publicised wedding.

"I'm afraid so, Juan. I didn't mean for it to happen. I never dreamed of such a thing. But lately, especially since I've become betrothed, it's as if something has changed, as though I see life differently. It has nothing to do with you," she added hastily. "It's just that I think my feelings were already engaged before all this happened. I just wasn't aware of it."

"And who is the man?" he asked, frowning. Then suddenly he remembered. "I know!" he exclaimed, looking her straight in the eye. "It's Pablito Sanchez, isn't it?" He brought his hand down on his thigh. "I should have guessed the other night, when I found him here with you in the study. What a damn fool I've been." He let out a laugh and shook his head. "My God, Letti, what a pair we are, you and I."

"Wh-what do you mean?" she whispered, astonished. "You mean you're not angry? You don't mind?"

"Angry?" he said, rising. "Why, Letti, it's the best news I've had in goodness knows how long. If you only knew what I've been through these past weeks—the agony, the—Sorry," he said raising his hands and smiling ruefully, "as you said, it has nothing to do with you."

"I think I know too," she said, a slow smile dawning through her tears. "It's Georgiana, isn't it?"

"How did you know?" Juan gazed down at her, eyes narrowed in surprise.

"Well, first I wondered when she turned up on my doorstep looking so exhausted—that night when you arrived and found her here. You looked so put out. But then she told me some nonsense about a boy at the university and I bought it. I thought I must have been wrong. Oh, gosh. Is that why she went home and sent me some pathetic excuse not to be my bridesmaid? Oh, Juan, how simply awful for the poor girl. I feel dreadful. If only I'd known I could have saved both of you so much heartache."

"Don't, Letti. Thank heavens you've told me what you just have." He squeezed her hands in his, and then, letting them go, smiled ruefully into her eyes. "You do realise, though, that under the circumstances we really can't be married."

"I know we *shouldn't*. But how can we not? Think of the scandal. My mother. *Dios mio*. Everything is arranged—the wedding, the dresses, the invitations sent out. I dread to think what hell my life would be if I refused to marry you."

"Now, don't get agitated. All we have to do is tell them the truth," he exclaimed, grabbing her hands in his again. "Tell them that you love Pablito and I love Georgiana. Surely they'll understand?"

"Oh, right." Leticia laughed witheringly. "I can just see my mother's face when I tell her I'm dumping one of the handsomest, wealthiest, most noble men in the realm for a socialist law lecturer with no background whatsoever, whose main ambition in life is to promote student awareness of socialist causes!" she exclaimed.

"You have a point," Juan admitted, grimacing. "I don't suppose if I talked to them it would help?"

"What? Tell them you're madly in love with one of the bridesmaids?" Leticia laughed, then sniffed and accepted his hanky gratefully. "You know, up until a few seconds ago I had a pretty good opinion of your intellect, Juan. Now

I'm beginning to wonder what you're on!" she said, laughing through her tears and recovering some of her old self-confidence.

"But, Letti, we have to do something. Come up with some excuse they'll buy. But first let's have a drink," he said, jumping up and pulling her with him. "We deserve one after all our troubles."

"Good idea," she agreed, taking his hand.

"Can you imagine what would have happened if you hadn't spoken tonight?" he said suddenly, pulling her close and holding her in a hug. "It's wonderful that we're good enough friends to be open with one another. Or rather, you *were* my friend," he said truthfully. "You're not upset I didn't tell you about Georgiana, are you?"

"No, silly," she said, reaching up and dropping a kiss on his cheek. "I'm sure you were being discreet and loyal for all the wrong reasons—which you'd convinced yourself were the right ones, like sacrificing love on the altar of duty and all that."

"That pretty well sums it up," he agreed, grinning. "Tell me, what kind of champagne do you keep in the house? You'd better get out your best bottle, Letti. This calls for a celebration."

"Don't put the cart before the horse," she warned. Then, suddenly laughing hysterically, she grabbed his arm. "I was just wondering what all our friends would say if they could see us now, rummaging about for a bottle of vintage champagne to celebrate the breaking of our engagement." She burst into another fit of uncontrollable laughter.

It took them a full five minutes to find the bottle, recover from their mirth and sit down, the cork popped and their glasses filled, to get a concrete game plan together.

* * *

Georgiana came out of her first ultrasound scan clutching the hazy image of a blob.

Her blob.

Her baby.

Seeing the blurred image made it all become real. The being who up until now had been a concept had become a person—to whom, henceforth, she was going to dedicate her life. She had already written to the university telling them she would not be returning. But the problem now was where to go?

She was still pretending to her mother that she wanted to study somewhere else in Europe, and although she knew she was lying to herself, as well as her parent, she still did not feel ready to face the consequences of revealing the truth. She needed time. Time on her own. Time to get used to the idea of becoming a single mother. Time to grieve for Juan and the love affair that was never to be.

Back at Wilton Crescent, Georgiana sat in her room and glanced at the calendar. Only a week left now until Juan's wedding to Leticia. She let out a long, sad sigh. It seemed desperately cruel that so many lives should be blighted in the name of duty. But she, Georgiana reflected, sitting up straighter, was damned if she'd surrender anything else to duty right now.

At least if she found somewhere to go on her own she could dream about him, think about him, miss him in peace without being told what a dreadful, irresponsible dirt-bag he was. Because that was exactly how her mother would view the man who'd apparently left her daughter pregnant and alone. Forget the fact that he wasn't even aware that she was carrying his baby. Lady Cavendish would only reason with a mother's love.

Georgiana smiled suddenly, placing her hand on her belly. Maybe one day she'd feel exactly the same. Perhaps some day, way down the years, the child now inside her would have similar feelings for someone and—

She broke off and made herself return to planning the upcoming months. She must come up with a scheme. Something to take care of the near future. The rest—how to tell her mother and all that—she'd worry about later.

Once Juan was married.

She realised suddenly that there lay the crux of the matter. Only once she knew it was a *fait accompli*, that there was no changing it, no going back—once she'd read all the newspaper reports, seen all the glossy magazine pictures—would she be able to recognise the devastating truth. Then it would sink in and she would finally let go and face reality.

But right now knowing she was losing the man she would love for ever was more than she could bear.

CHAPTER SEVENTEEN

"WHAT do you mean, you and Juan are breaking off your engagement?" Doña Elvira, Letti's mother, squeaked hysterically, before sinking onto the nearest chair, looking as though she was about to faint.

Horrified looks were exchanged around the drawing room in the Avenida Castellana, as Juan, standing next to Letti, broke the devastating news to their families.

"But this is preposterous," Don Alvaro spluttered, his face turning a dark shade of crimson. "Unheard of."

"Papà, please—it is a mutual decision," Letti pleaded, thankful for the support of Juan's arm. "Juan and I are very fond of each other as friends, but we are not in love. We don't feel our marriage would work."

"But what on earth does *love* have to do with it?" her mother asked weakly.

"Everything."

To everyone's surprise the Condessa's voice broke into the cacophony of protests and they turned in surprise.

"What can you possibly mean?" the Marquesa said in a querulous voice. "This is perfectly scandalous. You know as well as I do that love and marriage are not synonymous. Anyway, it is too late to cancel," she said on a stronger note, her lips set in a thin line. "The invitations have been sent out, the table placements arranged. I can't begin to tell you the work and the trouble, not to mention the dishonour to both our families..." She waved a trembling hand.

"And as for you, Letti, you are a most ungrateful, selfish daughter to even think of cancelling the wedding."

"Quite right, my dear," Don Alvaro agreed, puffing out his chest and sending Juan an angered look that expressed his feelings far better than words. "It is not fitting for you to be behaving in this absurd, ill-bred manner. Both of you know perfectly well that this marriage is most suitable. Pull yourselves together and let us hear no more of this ludicrous nonsense."

"But, Papà, it isn't ludicrous nonsense," Letti repeated, her voice surprisingly controlled, considering the brave step she was taking. "Please listen to what the Condessa has to say."

"And what is that?" Don Alvaro turned towards the Condessa, his eyes blazing.

"All I want to say is this," the Condessa said, assuming command of the situation. She sat poised and elegant in a pale blue chiffon dress and the de la Caniza diamond necklace that she'd insisted Juan take out of the safe for the occasion. "I think it is time we realised life has changed, Alvaro. Things are not as they were in our young day. It is entirely wrong for two young people to be forced into a loveless match for the sake of pride and duty."

"But they are not so young! They are both thirty and should know better," the Marquesa protested.

"And," the Condessa continued, ignoring the interruption with a raised brow, "things take on a different aspect when we consider that both parties happen to be in love with other people."

"What? In love with other people? What nonsense is this?" Don Alvaro muttered, dabbing his hanky to his forehead. "Letti's not in love. She's far too old for that kind of thing."

"Really? Perhaps you should get to know your daughter

better, Alvaro. Do stop being so pompous and for once in your life think of your daughter's happiness rather than your family pride.''

''Well, I never in all my life—''

''As I was saying,'' the Condessa continued, seemingly oblivious, ''Leticia is in love with a charming young man who was made known to me several days ago. He is not noble, and neither will he correspond to your expectations of a son-in-law. But it is my belief that he and Letti will live very happily together. And revolutionise the university,'' she added with a twinkling smile. ''They will lead worthwhile and fulfilled lives.''

''Revolutionise the uni—? But this is far worse than we imagined. *Dios mio, que catastrophe,*'' Doña Elvira wailed, leaning on her husband's arm for support.

''As for Juan,'' the Condessa finished, with an affectionate glance at her young cousin, ''he will also seek his happiness. But that is another story which I am not about to get into here.''

''This is outrageous,'' Don Alvaro hissed, and, turning towards Letti, let loose his rage. ''You are a blight on the family escutcheon—a dishonour to our reputation. I shall wipe you from the family records, young lady,'' he menaced, wagging a trembling finger at Letti. ''Your name shall never be mentioned again in my hearing. I shall abolish it. And I shall personally see to it that this—this creature—this upstart—this—this commoner with whom you have allied yourself behind our backs is removed from his employment, wherever that is, and—''

''Don Alvaro, I hesitate to interrupt you,'' Juan said in a cold, autocratic voice, ''but I have already told Leticia that any support she needs, be it financial or otherwise, she shall have from me. If you turn her out, you will only be making a fool of yourself. The whole of Madrid will talk.

Plus, Letti is quite capable of maintaining herself on her own. As for her future husband, he also has my full support. A new department at the university is about to be built, of which he will be the dean. His work is magnificent, and recognised by academics of the highest level both here and abroad. The King and Queen have visited one of his pet projects and offered their full approval,'' he added as a clincher.

''And if you take my advice, my dear Elvira,'' the Condessa added, leaning towards the Marquesa, ''you will pretend to the world that this union has your blessing. Think what fools you'd appear otherwise. Make it into a fairy-tale romance rather than the scandal of the season. Now, go home and rest, my dear. I realise this has been a great shock to you both,'' she added kindly, ''but I'm afraid we must move with the times. I'm sure that at heart neither of you would wish to see two such lovely people living unhappily together. Now, would you?'' She raised a silver brow.

''Come, my dear,'' Don Alvaro said, mustering all his dignity. ''We obviously have no place here. The Condessa is right. We must consider what is best to be done to stop our names being dragged in the mud.''

''But what about the lovely invitations? And the cake? And the scandal that will inevitably ensue?'' The Marquesa moaned, leaning on her husband's arm for support, tears welling in her eyes.

''Oh, dear. I knew I shouldn't have done it,'' Letti said in a hoarse whisper as her parents left. She made as though to run and support her mother, but Juan stopped her.

''If you show one iota of weakness now, you've had it,'' he hissed, holding her arm in a firm grip.

''But, Juan, I feel so awful. Look what I've done. I should have—''

''Don't,'' he replied, a hard edge to his voice. ''They were quite happy for you to sell yourself to the highest bidder so long as it satisfied their ambitions. Now, you make damn sure you satisfy yours. Oh, and I promised Pablito that you would phone him the minute this was all over,'' he added, to distract her. ''Here, take my cellphone and pop into the study.'' With a gentle shove, he pushed her towards the door.

Once they were alone, the Condessa let out a sigh and smiled. ''Well, Juan, that was quite an ordeal. Poor Letti. I hope they think this over properly and see what absolute fools they'll make of themselves if they don't give the girl their support. I'm sure in the end it will all work out. But tell me, *querido*, now that matters are taken care of on that front, how do you plan to sort yourself out?''

But before he could answer Letti returned with an incredulous Pablito, who, hardly believing his luck, had been waiting outside the building so he could personally extend his thanks to Juan and the Condessa. It was only after the two had been sent on their way, starry-eyed, still not quite believing that life had given them this incredible break, that he was able to answer the older woman's question.

''Oh, don't worry, *Tia*. I will of course phone Georgiana very shortly. And I'm sure that in a matter of days everything will be sorted out.'' He winked, then leaned down and dropped a kiss on her brow. ''You were wonderful, *Tia*. How can I ever thank you?''

''By getting your life in order,'' she said, sending him a thoughtful look.

It was just like Juan to believe that now everything had sorted itself out at his end Georgiana and any other problems would fall smoothly into place at his command. As he left the room, a tiny smile hovered about her lips.

He had a lot to learn still, she realised ruefully, and had the funny feeling he might be in for a rude surprise.

It was after a casual glance in the window of a travel agent's that Georgiana came up with the idea of a house somewhere she could be entirely alone. She knew she had to get away, go somewhere isolated, where she could think, reassess, get her ducks in a row. And the picture of a Tuscan villa seemed perfect.

As soon as she got home she went online and checked out several sites offering holiday villas for rent. As it was low season there were lots of good deals to be had, and by the end of the afternoon she'd discovered her dream house, an hour out of Florence in the Tuscan countryside. By early evening Georgiana had booked her flight, and the next morning, to her mother's complete surprise and indignation, she had packed her bags and left for the airport, certain that she was doing the right thing.

She desperately needed the solitude a villa in the tiny Tuscan village would afford her. Somewhere that held no memories, no reminders of Juan. No painful regrets wherever she turned.

As the plane landed at Florence's airport, Georgiana felt a rush of excitement. The first rush of anything she'd experienced since beginning the countdown to Juan's wedding day, she recognised. Now at least she'd have new thoughts to occupy her over the following days. There would be people to meet. Shops to be discovered, the countryside to investigate. Activities which she prayed would keep her too busy to think. This was definitely the first step on the road to healing her broken heart.

Her rental car was waiting for her on arrival, as were instructions on how to reach the villa. Two hours later, driving into the Tuscan hills, Georgiana felt certain she'd taken the right decision.

She drove past vineyards that in spring and summer would burgeon with new life, through sleepy hamlets basking in the late-afternoon sun, on until she reached the tiny village of Gianella. Entering the village, she parked in the cobblestoned *piazza*, and, opening her organiser, looked up the address of Signora Bagnoli, the landlady who would entrust her with the keys to the property.

The village was very small. Smiling at the nearest passerby—a large woman clad in shapeless black, holding the hand of a lively little boy who talked non-stop—Georgiana asked for directions to Signora Bagnoli's house. According to the kind villager, it was the second on the left past the *piazza*. Making her way there, Georgiana lifted her face and looked about her, enjoying the seventeenth-century architecture, the wrought-iron balconies, and drawing in her breath at the beauty of the last rays of sunshine bathing the imposing church tower that dominated the square.

People walked at a leisurely pace, chatting to one another, sending curious glances in her direction and occasionally smiling. Despite being on her own in a foreign place, Georgiana approached the house the woman had indicated convinced she'd been right to come. Here she could hide, lick her wounds, and face whatever lay up ahead in her own time. There would be no one to criticise, no one to demand or dictate.

And nothing to remind her of Juan.

Stepping up to the ancient hewn-wood door, she banged the bronze knocker and waited. A minute later a young woman in jeans and a T-shirt appeared at the door.

"Hello," Georgiana said, astounded to see that the young woman didn't look at all Italian. "I'm Georgiana Cavendish."

"Hi," the girl answered in perfect English, "I'm Patsy Bagnoli. Come on in."

"Are you English?" Georgiana asked, surprised.

"Yes." The girl laughed, shaking her long chestnut hair and smiling, blue eyes twinkling merrily. "I married an Italian artist. We live here in the village. The villa used to belong to Carlo's parents. Renting it out gives us some extra income. We're so glad you're planning to stay for a while. It'll be such fun to have someone English to talk to," she added, taking Georgiana into a marvellous low-beamed kitchen where herbs, straw-covered bottles of Chianti and hams hung in profusion over an ancient stove, reminding her of the *tasca* on the road to Seville.

Suppressing any nostalgia, Georgiana sat down at the kitchen table. Patsy produced a bottle of wine and two glasses. "Welcome to Tuscany," she said. "I'm sure you'll love the villa. I just hope you won't be too lonely up there on your own. Still, you'll see the neighbours and villagers will make sure you're all right."

Georgiana asked for a glass of water. She did not want to drink alcohol as she knew it could be bad for the baby. It was weird to be so conscious of another being growing inside her, but so it was. Now that she'd decided to keep the baby, her every thought was for its well-being.

The girls chatted a while, and Georgiana felt good that her landlords were a young couple whom she could relate to.

"I'll take you up to the house before it gets dark," Patsy said, taking a large bunch of rusty keys from a crooked nail planted in the centuries-old whitewashed wall.

Ten minutes later they were heading along an earth road among the vineyards.

"There it is." Patsy pointed ahead and Georgiana slowed the car to enjoy her first view of the Villa Collina, sitting majestically up on a small hill overlooking the vineyards and the rolling hills.

''It's lovely,'' she whispered, tears filling her eyes.

For all at once she could not help wondering what it would have been like had she come here with Juan, instead of alone. Then she quickly reminded herself that Juan was not an option. In a question of hours he would be married to Leticia, and all they'd shared would be dead and buried for ever.

Banishing the thought, Georgiana smiled at Patsy and they drove the last kilometre up to the house. The girl was talking excitedly, telling her details about the house and the garden, and Mariella, the lady who came in and cleaned twice a week.

''We thought you'd probably be a bit lost this first day, so we wondered if you'd like to come down to the village and have supper at our place?'' Patsy said as they reached the lovely terracotta building, its sagging tiles and gentle pink hue all that Georgiana had anticipated.

''Thank you, I'd love to,'' she said, accepting the invitation, grateful not to be by herself on her first night. For, although it was delicious to be here on her own, it was also daunting to know that she and the tiny bit of life inside her had no one but themselves to look to if anything went wrong.

Several minutes later Georgiana had been shown all the features and specifics of the house. Where the linen cupboard was, how the electricity and the gas worked. And Patsy had given her a list of phone numbers to call in case of any emergency.

''You've been wonderful,'' Georgiana exclaimed after they'd finished the tour. ''I don't know how to thank you.''

''My pleasure,'' the other girl replied, smiling. ''Now, I'll wait while you unpack and shower, and then we can return together to the village and meet Carlo for a drink in the *piazza* before dinner. You'll see—soon you'll be a part of this place."

"Thank you." Georgiana turned and walked up the stairs with tears in her eyes. She had not expected such a warm welcome from strangers. Somehow it touched the increasingly sensitive part of her being. Her emotions seemed so acute these days.

Bracing herself, she unpacked her suitcase, walked into the shower, and afterwards prepared to become a part of her new home.

"I'm afraid I don't have her address," Lady Cavendish answered Juan's enquiry. "All I have is the name of the village. But you have her cellphone number, don't you? I'm so sorry, Juan, that Georgiana desisted from being your bridesmaid. It was really very rude to decline at the last minute. I hope Leticia wasn't upset."

"There is no need to be sorry, Lady Cavendish. As it happens, the wedding has been cancelled."

"Cancelled? Good gracious, I'm so sorry. I had no idea. I was preparing to make the trip."

"I know. And I'm sorry. But I assure you it was for the best. Both Leticia and I feel we've taken the right decision, and we are happy about it."

"Well...' Lady Cavendish murmured, not quite knowing what to say. "As long as you're all happy with your choices then I'm sure it's for the best. As for Georgiana, she's off to some place in Tuscany that I've never heard of. You'd be best to try her mobile, as I said."

"I already have. She doesn't seem to be picking up her messages. I'm afraid I can only get through to her voicemail."

''Well, in that case I really don't know how to help you. Is it something urgent?''

Juan hesitated. He didn't know how much Georgiana had told her mother. By the looks of it, not much. ''Not urgent, exactly, just something I wanted to talk over with her. I wonder, where precisely is this village you mentioned?'' he asked casually, wondering what the hell Georgiana had gone to a Tuscan village for.

''Oh, if you hold on a minute I'll find the name,'' Lady Cavendish murmured. He could hear the rustle of paper as she flipped through notes. ''Ah. Here we are. It's called Gianella. Never heard of it. But apparently it's about an hour or so from Florence. I hope that may be of some help to you.''

''Yes. Of course. Thank you very much, Lady Cavendish. And if Georgiana happens to phone, would you tell her that I called and ask her to get in touch with me as soon as possible?''

''Certainly. But I have no idea when that will be. I'm afraid Georgiana's behaviour of late has been erratic, to say the least.''

As he laid down the phone Juan experienced a moment's irritation. He'd been certain Georgiana would be at home in London. That all he'd have to do was jump on a plane and be with her in a couple of hours. Now the process had become more complicated. Gianella. He looked at the name and frowned. What in God's name could have induced her to go to an Italian village in the middle of nowhere?

Just when he most needed her to be available.

It was frustrating not being able to tell her the news, let her know that all their problems were resolved, that at last they could be together. Wipe away the pain and sorrow he was certain she must be experiencing and plan their future.

Juan sighed, swivelled in his office chair and tried Georgiana's mobile number again. Only to end up with the same monotonous voicemail message. He supposed if she didn't answer her phone any time soon it would mean travelling to Gianella himself. At least the initial rumpus over the cancellation of the wedding had died down now, and he could take a few days off without letting Letti down.

Georgiana checked her messages. When she saw several calls from Juan listed, she swallowed. It was typical, she thought, angered now, that on his wedding day he should be phoning *her*.

What for? she wondered, gripped by fury and frustration. To turn the knife in the wound? Surely he must realise how much it hurt her to know he was marrying another woman? She didn't need to be reminded of it again and again.

Throwing the phone down on the gnarled kitchen table, Georgiana determined not to think about him or the wedding.

Going about her business, she picked up one of the pretty wicker baskets hanging on the kitchen wall and went out into the herb garden. Its subtle aroma soothed her frazzled nerves as she concentrated on what herbs to pick for the dish she planned to cook for Patsy and Carlo.

Dinner on the night she'd arrived had proved great fun with her new English friend and her delightful husband, a painter, in their gorgeous village house. For the first time in weeks Georgiana had truly relaxed and enjoyed herself. Now, three days later, and installed in the villa, she wanted to return the hospitality. At least cooking and preparing a meal for her guests would take her mind off thc wedding, stop her from counting the hours, from constantly glancing at her watch, imagining exactly what stage the wedding preparations had reached.

Six o'clock.

And the wedding was planned for eight.

And there was Juan, cheerfully phoning *her* only hours before he took his vows with another woman. The thought left her seething. She wanted to weep with impotent rage.

How cynical could he get? she wondered, savagely snipping stalks of basil, her fingers shaking as she tossed them into the basket. How dared he play fast and loose with Leticia *and* her? She didn't care how much a marriage of convenience—or whatever he liked to call it—the ceremony was. At least he could have the decency to be loyal to his bride on their wedding day.

In fact, Georgiana decided, marching back towards the kitchen, she was actually very well rid of him.

As she opened the back door her phone rang again. In her agitated state she picked it up without checking the number.

''Georgiana, *querida*—at last.''

She froze, dropped the basket, and held the edge of the table, hit by a sandstorm of feelings rushing unbridled to the fore: anger, pain, rage, longing—all soared within her.

''How dare you?'' she cried, cutting him off mid-sentence. ''How do you have the audacity to ring me when in less than two hours you'll be marrying Leticia?'' she hissed, hands trembling. ''You're beyond belief, Juan, totally unscrupulous. I hate you. I never want to hear from you again—ever,'' she ended, tears stifling her voice as she turned off the phone and threw it into the fallen basket of herbs, before sinking onto the nearest chair and collapsing in a flood of tears.

What on earth was the matter with her? Hadn't Lady Cavendish told her the wedding was off? And to make it worse Georgiana hadn't allowed him to speak. *Dios mio*, what a damn mess. Juan paced his study, worried, pressing the repeat button on his cellphone for the umpteenth time, hoping beyond hope that Georgiana would pick up and allow him to explain what was going on before judging him so harshly. There must be some way of explaining to her that she was mistaken, that he had no intention of marrying Letti.

That he intended to marry her.

It was so obvious, so cut and dried for him. But of course if she still believed he was marrying Letti that explained it. Of course, he consoled himself confidently, as soon as she knew the truth everything would be resolved.

When finally he gave up ringing Juan sat down and called his secretary. The best thing to do was make immediate travel arrangements. The sooner he got to Gianella and made Georgiana listen to reason, the better it would be. Then matters would be settled and life could move on.

After reserving a first-class ticket to Italy, Juan felt better. It would of course be easy once he reached the village to find her. And after that there would be no problem making her see the light. He smiled. It was natural for her to have been angry that he'd phoned if she still believed he was marrying another woman. But all that would be easily smoothed over as soon as he arrived and explained matters.

He glanced at his watch. He would have to get ready if he was going to be on the evening flight to Rome, where he would connect to Florence.

Rising, Juan marched confidently to his apartments. There he found his valet. After instructing the man on what he needed for the journey, Juan went in search of the Condessa. With a bit of luck Georgiana could be persuaded to return with him. She could stay here under the Condessa's chaperonage while they made plans for the future. All in all, life would work out very well.

With a smile and a nod Juan entered the living room, content in the knowledge that from now on it would all be plain sailing.

CHAPTER EIGHTEEN

BY THE time Juan drove the last few miles to Gianella the following day he was tired, irritated, and glad to be arriving at his journey's end. First the flight from Madrid had been delayed due to bad weather. Then in Rome he'd been obliged to hire a plane to get him to Florence, since all the internal airlines were on strike that day.

Now, at last, he'd reached the village. All he needed was for one of the residents to give him directions to Georgiana's villa and then he'd have reached his destination and the woman he loved. It was still unclear to him why she should have chosen to bury herself in the middle of the Tuscan countryside, but so be it. That also was something he planned to rectify very promptly.

He had a number of ideas on how to spend the next few days. A lot of hours, he hoped, a smile ghosting on his lips, would be spent in bed, loving her, catching up, caressing her as he'd dreamed of so often over the past weeks.

Arriving in the *piazza*, he parked the smart Alfa Romeo he'd picked up at the airport and made his way across the street to the nearest bar.

"Ah, you are looking for the *signorina* Inglesa?" The bartender nodded, leaning across the old wood and marble counter to answer his enquiry. *"La signorina, e bellissima,"* the man enthused, kissing his fingers in an expressive gesture.

"Per piacere," Juan replied, smiling, and ordered a *café machiatto.* "Do you know where I might find her?"

"Va bene." The man rubbed his brow thoughtfully, then turned towards the coffee machine and shrugged in a manner only Italians knew how. "She might be at the Villa Collina. On the other hand she might be with the other Inglesa."

"What other Inglesa?"

"Signora Patsy. Another lovely example of womanhood. Carlo the artist's wife," the man said, in a tone that implied Juan should know these obvious facts. Then he laid down the coffee on the bar with a flourish.

"Who is she? The other lady, I mean?" Juan asked, wondering if Georgiana had come with a friend. Lady Cavendish hadn't mentioned her travelling with anyone else. In fact he'd got the impression Lady C was annoyed that Georgiana was on her own.

"The *signora* Inglesa lives over there, in that house you can see to the left. The one with the dark wooden shutters." The man pointed across the *piazza* down to a house in a nearby street.

Downing his coffee, Juan placed a note on the counter and, thanking the man for his assistance, headed across the square to the house, where he knocked smartly on the door. Seconds later it was opened by an attractive chestnut-haired girl with big blue eyes.

"Hi, I'm sorry to bother you," he said, smiling his seductive lazy smile, "but I'm looking for Georgiana Cavendish. The man at the bar seemed to think you might know where I could find her."

The girl sent him a speculative look. "And who are you?" she asked coldly.

Juan felt like telling her it was none of her damn business. Then, realising that wouldn't get him very far, he smothered his pride. ''I'm an old friend of hers. Juan Monsanto. I've come to pay her a visit.''

''Really?'' The girl raised a brow and looked him up and down in what Juan considered a most impertinent manner. ''Are you sure Georgiana wants to see you?''

''Look, this is a ridiculous conversation,'' he said, losing his patience. ''Kindly tell me where I can find Georgiana. It's very important. I need to speak to her at once.''

''The point,'' Patsy replied, crossing her arms firmly, ''is not whether you want to see her, but if *she* wants to see *you.*''

''I can't think why she shouldn't,'' he exclaimed angrily.

''Can't you?''

''Look, I don't mean to be rude, Signora, but frankly my reasons for wanting to see Georgiana are none of your business.''

''Sir, you made them my business when you came knocking at my door asking for her. Georgiana happens to be my friend. From her description of you I get the strong impression you're the last person on the planet she wants to see.''

Juan stood in patent astonishment as the door was summarily slammed in his face. He was about to lift his hand to knock again angrily when a hand came down on his shoulder.

''I wouldn't do that if I was you.''

He spun round to meet the amused dark gaze of a young Italian man of medium height, smiling ruefully.

''What have you to do with this?'' Juan snapped. He'd had just about enough of people interfering in his personal life for one day.

''Oh, I'm her husband,'' Carlo said, with a smile and a jerk of the head towards the reverberating door. ''Terrible temper, that one, when she loses it. I heard you were looking for Georgiana?"

"Yes," Juan muttered in a measured tone, "I am. I don't suppose *you* can tell me where I can find her?"

"I might," Carlo responded, the slow smile spreading across his handsome features. "But I suggest we cross the road and have a drink first. I get the feeling my *bellissima* Patsy may have her wires crossed. She can be very loyal and passionate about friendship. It's one of the things I like about her," he added with a wink, and a nod in the direction of the bar. "But you know women—they sometimes don't see things in their proper perspective."

"How very true," Juan replied with feeling. Slipping off his jacket, he threw it over his shoulder and fell into step with this young man who at least seemed open to helping him. "I'm Juan Monsanto," he said, stretching out his hand.

"Carlo Bagnoli. *Piacere.*"

The two men strode across the *piazza* and entered the bar. Juan ordered a cold beer and Carlo a Negroni.

"So, you're the wicked lover who dumped Georgiana for another woman," Carlo said, raising his glass and taking a long, appraising sip.

"What?" Juan's head jerked up in astonishment. "*Dios mio.* Is that how she sees me?"

"That's pretty much how it came over when Patsy described the story to me. Aren't you meant to be married and on your honeymoon or something?"

"Yes. No. I damn well am not." Juan brought the glass down on the table with a bang and let out an oath. "This is all perfectly ridiculous."

"Must be some kind of confusion," Carlo said, taking another long sip. "Pasty got the impression you were on your way to some exotic island with your bride."

"Look, this is absurd. The truth is, I was going to marry someone else, but we called off the wedding as we both realised we were in love with other people. Please, Carlo, I must see Georgiana at once and tidy up this terrible misunderstanding."

"Well, if you like I can show you the way to the villa."

"Finally." Juan cast his eyes to heaven, then smiled at his new friend. "I don't know how to thank you enough. God, women can be difficult."

"Can't they just?" Carlo rolled his eyes as Juan slapped a note down on the table and the two men made their way out into the night.

The flash of headlights made Georgiana look up from the book she'd been trying to concentrate upon unsuccessfully for the past half-hour. Laying it down on the coffee-table, Georgiana rose and, moving into the ample hall of the villa, went to the window next to the front door.

Who could possibly be visiting her at this hour? Carlo and Patsy hadn't said they were coming over this evening.

For a moment a flash of anxiety gripped her. Then she pulled herself together. Nothing happened in Gianella that the neighbours didn't know all about. Somebody would have seen a strange car passing through the village. Georgiana warily opened the door, unable to distinguish the vehicle in the glare of headlights.

Juan saw her as she stood, eyes narrowed, trying to tell who was coming, her beautiful long blonde mane flowing about her shoulders, her face etched in the glow of the headlights. Slowly he came to a stop only a few feet from where she stood. Then, before she had a chance to take in who it was, he switched off the car's engine, jumped out and crossed the few steps that separated them before she could react.

"*Mi amor,*" he muttered in a low growl, taking her possessively into his arms. "At long last I've found you."

"Juan!" she cried, straining in his arms and pulling away. "What are you doing here? How dare you come here? You have no right to disturb my peace. Don't you have any feelings for anyone? Surely even you didn't have the nerve to leave Leticia on her honeymoon and come looking for another woman?" she spat.

"Georgiana, if you'll just let me explain I—"

"Explain? I despise everything about you." She drew back into the safe angle of the open door and looked him over, her eyes filled with hot anger.

"Georgiana, if you'd at least allow me to explain," he repeated, "perhaps you'd understand that none of what you're saying makes any sense." He spoke calmly, raising his arms and moving towards her.

"Oh, doesn't it?" she jeered, throwing her hair back, eyes blazing. "Don't think you can come here cajoling me with your sweet talk, Juan. I've had enough. I know how you operate and I'm not prepared to tolerate it. You're a married man. Go back to your wife."

As she made to slam the door in his face he caught it, moving so swiftly she couldn't counter it.

"You have a pretty poor opinion of me if this is what you think," he threw harshly, grabbing her arm as her hand swung towards his cheek. "Oh, no, *señorita*, I will not allow any temper tantrums. And now, like it or not, you will listen to me," he said, pinning her arms to her sides.

"Leave me alone," she said, overwhelmed, hot tears rushing to her eyes as he held her fast. "I won't listen to a word you have to say. I can't believe you've come here," she said, breaking down, crumpling.

Juan held her, shocked, but determined to have his way.

"*Amor mio*, please—just hear me out." In one swift

movement he swept her into his arms and entered the house, moving instinctively towards the living room.

A fire blazed in the huge stone hearth and the soft glow of lamplight encompassed the low-beamed room. Juan sat down on the couch, still holding her in his arms.

"I will not let go of you until you hear everything I have to say," he insisted, feeling her struggle. Then, before she could react further, he pressed his lips on hers. His fingers smoothed her hair gently, and his hands coursed reassuringly down her back. "Georgiana," he whispered hoarsely, "my beautiful, wilful Georgiana. Did you really believe that I would come here to you straight from the arms of another woman?"

"You certainly had no qualms about it before," she murmured, wanting so hard to resist, but entranced by the scent of him, the delicious feel of his body cleaving to hers, the sheer delight of knowing his arms were around her.

"Georgiana, will you please listen for once? Leticia and I broke off our engagement."

"You *what*?" She sat up straight and perched on his knee, staring at him unbelieving.

"We broke off our engagement," he repeated patiently. "You see, it boiled down to this: both of us are in love with someone else."

"Leticia? In love with someone else?" she whispered amazed. "But who?"

"Pablito Sanchez, at the university. He'd never had the courage to speak his mind—thought she was too good for him and all that. But then, when he realised he was really going to lose her to someone else, everything came out and she realised she loved him. Poor Letti. She was so caught up between doing her duty to the family by marrying me and wishing she could follow her heart that she hardly had the courage to tell me."

"But you..." Georgiana said warily. "You would have gone through with the wedding anyway, wouldn't you?"

He hesitated, then, looking deep into her eyes, knew he must speak the truth. "Yes. I would. I almost told her the truth before she revealed her heart to me. But I couldn't. I felt it would be so utterly wrong, so hurtful. After all, I had offered her marriage. How could I go back on my word?"

"So you would have been prepared to marry her and carry on an affair with me? Is that right?"

"That isn't what I really wanted," he said, aware that he was treading on quicksand.

"No, but you would have done it all the same, wouldn't you?" she insisted, head high.

Juan sighed. This was harder than he'd expected. When she slipped from his arms and rose to stand near the fire he didn't stop her.

"Georgiana, I did what I had to do. Try and see this from my point of view. I am a man of honour. I couldn't break my word."

"Let me see if I understand you correctly," she said, the fire blazing in her large green eyes belying her conversational tone. "To tell Leticia the truth about us wasn't okay, but to carry on an affair behind her back was? I'm afraid I'm having a hard time understanding." She crossed her arms and looked him straight in the eye, pain and anger battling with the overwhelming desire to feel his arms about her, his body on hers.

Yet she knew that she mustn't. Couldn't. Would regret it for ever if she did. She had the baby to think of now. She couldn't give way to her own desires, but must think of the better good for them all.

Juan looked across at her, then into the flames. "I know you find it almost impossible to understand the way I was brought up. In England you think differently. But you see, had Leticia not been in love with another man, had she married me as planned, she never would have expected me to be faithful to her. This was no love match, Georgiana. Letti and I are friends, but we've never so much as exchanged more than a peck on the cheek. *Dios mio,*" he exclaimed, losing his patience as the desire to possess her engulfed him, "can't you see that it is all over? Finished? That all that is behind us, and now we can begin our life together?"

"*Our* life together?" She raised a startled brow. "What makes you think that I would want a life with you?"

"I thought—" He rose and moved towards her, opening his arms.

"No!" She held up her hand like a traffic cop, stopping him in his stride. "I never asked you for anything. I came here to think, to get my life sorted out. Not to be—to be coerced into something I—" She turned her back on him, shoulders heaving.

If only he knew the truth. But thank goodness he didn't. For if that were the case then she would have no choice. And right now, as much as she loved him, knew she wanted him, she had to come to terms with herself and the situation. What if even now all Juan wanted was a casual affair? After all, he'd only said "begin our life together". There had been no mention of marriage or permanence.

"I wish you would leave now," she said unsteadily. "I need time to myself, time to think."

"I can't believe this is the way you receive me," he said, taking another step forward.

"I suppose you expected me to fall into your arms and in with your wishes."

"Well, aren't they identical? Don't we want the same thing? Hell, Georgiana, all I can think of is making love to you. Isn't it the same for you?'' he asked quietly, his eyes burning into hers as slowly he approached her.

Georgiana stood her ground. But his presence was mesmerising. When he touched her cheek, trailed his fingers possessively down it, down her throat until he reached the swell of her breast, she wanted to protest, wanted to push him away. But she couldn't. Instead a smothered sigh of longing escaped her.

Without more ado, Juan pulled her roughly into his arms and his lips began their raid, a passionate, sensuous path of kisses feathering her face, her throat, up to her lips and back again, hands roaming, his thumb seeking her taut, aching nipples knowingly, until she cried out with suppressed longing.

Before she could protest he undressed her deftly. Not gently or kindly, but tearing the clothes from her, still expertly taunting and caressing her until she lay writhing on the rug before the hearth, sighing his name, begging for his tongue, his fingers to cover every inch of her flesh until she could bear it no more. Soon they were lying naked, their bodies entwined, sensing, touching, discovering once again their deep, unfettered need for one another, too overwhelming to deny.

Juan murmured to her softly, passionate words of love and desire that she barely understood but absorbed as his cunning fingers flicked her breasts again, wreaking their magic, before coursing tantalisingly south. When he finally reached between her thighs, rediscovered the throbbing heat she held hidden there, he sighed and, lowering his lips to her, set out to cause havoc, until, aching wildly, she was begging for him to bring her to completion.

Then and only then, when he was certain she was his for the taking, did he enter her, thrusting hard and possessive, delighting in the torrid damp heat of her.

Hips arching to meet him, Georgiana let out a cry of pain, love, fear and primal longing. For him, for her, for the child they had created in a similar act to this one.

When it was over he cradled her in his arms.

"I will never let you go," he muttered into her hair. "The past is the past. The future lies ahead. We can make of it what we want. It's up to us. The choices are ours for the taking."

"Are they?" she murmured, trailing her fingers across his broad tanned chest. "Do you really believe that we make all our choices?"

"Why, of course," he said arrogantly, moving her head back and staring down amused into her eyes. "We can do whatever we like now. Nothing and nobody can dictate to us what we should or shouldn't do. We're free, Georgiana. Nothing and nobody can stop us."

Georgiana heaved a sigh and moved away from him. "You make everything sound so easy," she said, gathering his shirt from the floor and slipping it over her.

Should she tell him the truth? Was this the moment to reveal her deepest, most precious secret? Was he ready to receive it, cherish it as she did? Or would he want her to—? The sudden thought that crossed her mind hurt so badly she cringed. And the truth was she didn't entirely trust him—not after he'd told her quite plainly that he would have been willing to go through with the wedding if Letti hadn't cried off.

Just remembering the words still left her cold inside.

And all at once she knew she needed more time.

Time on her own.

Just as he had taken decisions in his life, she had to take decisions in hers. Maybe it was wrong to deny their baby a father, but she could take care of their child by herself, she argued.

"Juan, I need to be alone," she said suddenly, turning away, pulling the shirt about her and moving towards the stairs. "There's a spare room upstairs. You can sleep in it for the night and we'll talk in the morning."

Then, running up the stairs before he could protest, she closed the bedroom door and threw herself onto the bed, too confused, too anguished to do more than lie there, hot tears seeping into her pillow.

Juan rose slowly. He couldn't believe her reaction. Why was she behaving in this strange manner? Surely it must be obvious to her that they had to be together? He'd held her in his arms, felt the passion of her orgasm. He knew she loved him. So what was all this ridiculous nonsense about? Surely she couldn't still be upset about his engagement? After all, it was something which had occurred before he'd even met her. The fact that he hadn't given his fiancée the boot had nothing to do with his true desires, and had been prompted only by his deep sense of honour. Surely Georgiana could understand and respect that now it was all over?

Angrily, Juan flung on his jeans and the jersey he'd been wearing and went in search of the kitchen. There he found a bottle of wine and a glass. Picking them up, he returned to the living room and, flinging his legs up on an old leather ottoman, sipped slowly, staring gloomily into the flames, wondering where to go from here. He was tired and hurt and disappointed at his reception. For a moment he glanced at the stairs, then thought better of it. Better let things be. In the morning they'd talk it over and hopefully she would be more reasonable.

Several hours later he woke and sat up stiffly. The fire was barely alive; only a few crackling embers shifted in the grate. He rubbed his eyes and glanced at his watch.

Two a.m. He'd better, he supposed, seek out the bed Georgiana had offered him, and try and get some sleep before sorting matters out in the morning.

Wearily Juan mounted the old wooden staircase. On the creaking landing he stopped and glanced at the doors. There was one closed one, which instinctively he sensed was Georgiana's. He hesitated. Should he go in? Hold her and try to put an end to this absurd situation? Or would he do better to wait until daylight to reason with her?

But as he was about to follow this last course of action and enter the other bedroom a moan from behind the closed door made him stop dead in his tracks. He listened carefully for a moment. Then he heard another. Without hesitating Juan flung open the door of her bedroom, shocked when he saw Georgiana curled in a ball on the bed, crying.

"*Mi amor!*" He rushed to the bed. "What is it? What is wrong, my love?"

"I—I think I'm losing it," she whispered, gripping her stomach as pain slashed through her once more.

"Losing what? What are you talking of?" Juan took her in his arms and held her to him, the sight of her pale face and obvious pain leaving him anguished.

"The baby," she said at last.

"The baby?" He looked at her blankly. Then all at once truth dawned and he gazed down at her in wonder. "You mean, you're pregnant—and you didn't tell me?"

"Yes," she whispered, convulsing once more. "I think something's happening. I need to get to a hospital."

Without more ado Juan lifted her in his arms and, kicking the door aside, rushed hastily down the stairs. Grabbing his keys from the pocket of his jeans, he carried her to the car, where he laid her carefully in the passenger seat before hurrying to the driver's seat and starting the engine.

"There must be a hospital near here somewhere," he muttered, desperate, unable to think straight. The news that she was carrying his child and that she might lose it if he didn't hurry to get her to safety warred in his agitated mind.

As the car rushed down the bumpy road towards the village Georgiana was in too much pain, too worried about her baby, to care that she'd just told Juan the truth. They screeched around the last corners, heading towards the village lights, and she suddenly remembered where the hospital was. She'd asked Patsy, knowing she needed to find a doctor for her prenatal care.

She directed Juan past the *piazza*, then on up a sharp incline to the top of the village, where a small but modern clinic had been built only five years earlier.

By the time they stopped in the car park Juan was paler than Georgiana. He jumped out of the car and came around to help her. Leaning against the car, she tried to take a few faltering steps but failed. The pain was excruciating. Without hesitation Juan scooped her up once more and carried her quickly to the entrance of the clinic.

"It'll be all right, *mi niña*," he muttered nervously as he hurried into the building.

Even though it was the middle of the night, the place was busy. A few people sat on plastic chairs near the entrance, obviously waiting to be treated.

"Per favore." Juan stopped a woman who looked like a doctor. "Please, we need immediate help. My wife is losing our baby."

The woman—dark-haired, bespectacled—reacted immediately. Next thing Georgiana knew she was being wheeled on a trolley with a nurse inserting a drip in her hand and Juan hurrying beside it. But all she could register were his words: *my wife*.

''Will she be all right, Doctor?'' he asked, never taking his eyes from Georgiana.

''I'm afraid it's too soon to say,'' the doctor said, placing a hand on his arm. ''Your wife is very pale, and her heart rate is too fast. I can only tell you after examining her.''

Your wife. Again the words echoed as Juan's lips touched her brow before she was wheeled into a small examination room.

Juan watched the doors close behind the trolley. He leaned back against the whitewashed wall and closed his eyes. His head drooped. If anything happened to her he would never forgive himself. No wonder she had been so distraught, so anguished.

She was carrying his child.

The thought both overwhelmed and excited him. He should have guessed something was different about her. All at once he worried that their passionate lovemaking had somehow caused the present problem. Then he dropped his head in his hands and wished he'd been less blind, less arrogant and less of a fool. So much for his duty and his honour. Right now the woman he loved and their child were in danger, and his duty lay right here—with them.

He'd been blind not to realise that Georgiana and their life together were more important than anything else. He hadn't bothered to understand what her feelings must be, believing he would sacrifice her for another woman. Or that the consequences of their lovemaking could end up like this.

Now all he prayed for was that both mother and child would be safe. The rest he could deal with.

An hour later he was still standing in the same position, waiting. At last the doors opened and the doctor reappeared.

''I'm happy to tell you that both mother and baby are

well,'' she said, smiling. ''I'm afraid she'll have to stay in for a couple of days, though—''

''Are you sure she's all right?'' Juan went pale as a sheet. If anything had happened to Georgiana he wouldn't be able to bear it.

''Your wife will be perfectly fine. And so will the child. But she must be very careful.''

''Oh, my God.'' Juan swallowed, horrified at how easily the good news could have turned tragic. What mattered above all was that Georgiana was safe.

''She should be fine in a few days,'' the doctor continued. ''That is, physically. Though she must take things easy and be monitored for the rest of her pregnancy. Of course you must be prepared for her to be fragile emotionally. She was shocked psychologically. She may feel very shaken for a while, and will need your full attention.''

''Of course, Doctor. *Grazie,*'' he said, recovering a semblance of normality. ''Can I see her?''

''I'm afraid she needs to rest until morning.'' Seeing Juan was about to protest, she continued, ''If you like, I can arrange for a collapsible bed to be put in the room.''

''Any chair will do,'' he said abstractedly, as the doctor led him down the corridor to the room where Georgiana had been wheeled.

Juan stepped quietly into the room. It was dark and quiet. Georgiana's pale face lay motionless on the pillow lit only by the moonlight filtering through the half-closed curtains.

Juan carefully took a chair and placed it next to the bed. Then, laying his hand over hers, he began a silent vigil. He would take care of her and their child, love them, and never let them go. And as soon as she was able to he would marry her—whether she liked it or not.

CHAPTER NINETEEN

GEORGIANA was woken by soft autumn sun dancing on the white hospital coverlet. She blinked. Then a slight pain in her abdomen reminded her of all that had happened the night before.

Opening her eyes, she saw Juan seated next to her, asleep in the chair, his hand still holding hers.

Tears flooded her eyes and caught in her throat. Thank God the baby was saved—her precious baby, the one for whom she was willing to sacrifice so much, even change her life.

Carefully she drew her hand out of Juan's, but the movement woke him and he stirred.

"*Mi amor…*" He yawned, shook his head and sat up next to her on the bed. "Are you all right, my love?"

She nodded silently, stifling the tears that for some reason surfaced.

"*Ay, mi niña,*" he said, folding her in his arms. "Cry, my darling. You have every right to. I have been a monster. But I am so glad you and the baby are safe. And this is just the first," he said, gazing into her eyes. "There will be many more babies. As many as you want," he murmured, a crooked smile covering his face as he stroked her hair. And Georgiana let the tears she'd been holding and all the pain of the past weeks go.

"Can you forgive me, little one? You know you should

have told me at once,'' he murmured, still holding her head close to his chest.

''Juan, I couldn't tell you,'' she whispered, her voice muffled against his sweater. ''Not when you were about to marry someone else.''

''I understand that, my darling. But now everything is different. You are going to marry me.''

''But—''

''No buts, Georgiana,'' he commanded, drawing her head back and looking at her, his eyes filled with love and determination. ''As soon as you can get out of this bed I will arrange for the local priest to marry us. I'm sure Carlo can arrange it.''

''But what about—?''

''Shush. I won't tolerate any dissension in the ranks,'' he said, kissing her mouth very thoroughly.

At that moment a knock on the door announced the arrival of Dottore Savona—the doctor who had attended Georgiana the night before.

''Good morning,'' she said, obviously amused to catch the couple romantically embracing. ''How are you feeling?''

''Better.'' Georgiana smiled shakily at the doctor. Then she asked the question that had been in her mind ever since waking. ''Doctor, are you sure the baby is okay?''

''Why, of course. What happened has not affected the baby in any way. You must rest, though, and take it easy until the birth. But I'm sure your husband will take care of you.''

''Future husband,'' Juan corrected with a wicked smile. ''Dottore, you can be the first to congratulate us. We are going to be married as soon as Georgiana can leave the hospital.''

''Ah, many congratulations,'' she said, shaking his hand

and smiling down at Georgiana. ''Are you planning a wedding here in the village?''

''Yes,'' Juan answered in an authoritative tone. ''And you are all invited.''

Georgiana was about to protest, to say that he was impossibly bossy and that she wanted to plan her wedding herself, when all at once she realised that this was exactly what she would like. Closing her eyes, she acquiesced. There would probably be quite a few battles and crossings of wills with Juan, but then that too was part of their relationship. Or maybe, she reflected, in the way women had, for as long as mankind had existed, she'd learn to manage him…

''Is that not an excellent plan?'' he said, turning towards the bed and looking down at her possessively.

''Excellent, my love. I couldn't have planned it better myself.''

Georgiana caught the doctor's wink and they exchanged a quiet smile. And, later, once the door was closed and Juan had taken her in his arms again, she knew that the baby had joined them in a way nothing else ever could.

''I will never leave you ever again,'' Juan declared, holding her tight.

''Nor I you,'' she said, adding with a touch of humour, ''After all, we don't know where your duty might lead you, do we?''

Look out for SAVANNAH SECRETS,
Fiona's newest title, published
under the MIRA® imprint in March.
Here we have an extract
for you to enjoy...

When eccentric Rowena Carstairs leaves her sizeable estate to an illegitimate grandson who was given up for adoption at birth, Savannah attorney Meredith Hunter is obliged to track him down. Her search takes her to the wilds of Scotland, where she is shocked to discover that the man is none other than infamous corporate raider Grant Gallagher...

Turn the page for more from
Fiona Hood-Stewart!

"GOOD morning. Is this Miss Hunter?"

"Speaking. I'm glad you finally called, Mr. Gallagher. I was getting worried you hadn't received my correspondence."

"Not only did I receive it, but I considered it a great piece of impertinence."

"Excuse me?" Meredith swallowed, aghast. "I'm afraid I don't understand."

"Then let me explain. I have no interest in Mrs. Carstairs's inheritance. I suggest you find yourself another heir, as I will not be accepting the bequest."

"But—"

"I also wish to make it abundantly clear that I do not want to be bothered with this matter, now or at any time in the future. I expect you to take care of any details. Am I making myself perfectly clear?" His voice grated, cold and unbending, down the line.

"Mr. Gallagher, it isn't quite as simple as that." Meredith bristled.

"I suggest you make it simple. I have no intention of cooperating, if that's what you're about to suggest. Good day, Miss Hunter. I'm sure you will deal efficiently with any necessary details."

"Wait," she threw out. "You can't just avoid the issue as if it doesn't exist. There are papers to sign, documents to be dealt with."

''Then deal with them. It's none of my damn business. Goodbye.''

The phone went dead in Meredith's hand. ''I don't believe this,'' she muttered, outraged. ''The guy just brushed me off like a fly. I knew I was right about the kind of person he is.''

''What did he say?'' Meredith's assistant Tracy prodded. She'd followed the conversation closely, had seen Meredith change colour, the growing glint in her eye.

''You know what? That's it.'' Meredith slapped her palms down on the desk, eyes blazing. ''I'm going after the bastard. Thinks he can just walk, does he? Well, he'll soon find out that ain't happening. Not on my watch.''

''Go girl. That's the spirit,'' Tracy encouraged, smothering a smile. Nothing like a challenge to get Meredith off her butt.

''Fine,'' Meredith muttered, slamming the Carstairs file down before her. ''If I have to go, I'll go to Scotland. Even if it does mean luring him out of his den. The nerve of it,'' she added, smoldering. ''The sheer rudeness of the man. I knew this was what he'd be like. Didn't I tell you?''

''Absolutely. The sooner you get going, the better. And since that takes care of that, I'll be off,'' Tracy answered, rising and straightening her skirt. ''It'll be fine. You'll see.''

''Damn right it will,'' Meredith answered, letting out another pent-up huff.

She already detested Grant Gallagher.